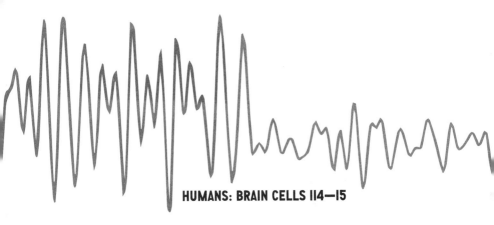

HUMANS. DEEP IN THE OLDEST JUNGLE. DENSE GREEN. BIRDCALLS echo. *Wet earth smell. Mud squishes through toes. Air thick enough to taste. Following a skeleton hiker. That suddenly lights up a network of sparking nerves, feeding into a glowing brain. A clearing ahead. There—a dark figure, from the future, stands on a mound of sand, winds up, and fires a rock . . . fast, faster, fastest . . . dreams Janegoodall.*

Candy. Sweet, sour, salty, bitter, hot, cold, glorious. Turbocharged candy. Pulsing, exploding super candy . . . dreams Watson.

The watery crash of ocean waves. Schools of . . . those fish . . . not really fish . . . what do you call those things? Bottlenose mammals leap out of the water in graceful arcs. The blue-green water covering Earth. The solar system of Mercury, Venus, Mars . . . and that next planet. Used to know them like my own name . . . dreams Grampa Al.

Purple storm clouds crashing over volcano lightning-bolt drumming heartbeat explosion. Grab that blue-white crackling electrical charge. Guide it into looping spiral. Multiply it through brain stem, to brain lobes in a beautiful, throbbing, golden network. Janegoodall cheers. Watson laughs. Grampa Al, but somehow ten-year-old Grampa Al, dances a funny little dance . . . dreams Frank Einstein.

OIOIOIII OIOOIOOO OIOIIOOI OOIOOOOO
OIOOOOII OIOOIOOO OIOOIOOI OIOOOOII
OIOOIOII OIOOOIOI OIOOIIIO OOIOOOOO
OIOIOIII OIOOIOOO OIOIIOOI OOIIIIII . . .
dreams Klink.

and the BRAINTURBO

JON SCIESZKA

ILLUSTRATED BY BRIAN BIGGS

AMULET BOOKS
NEW YORK

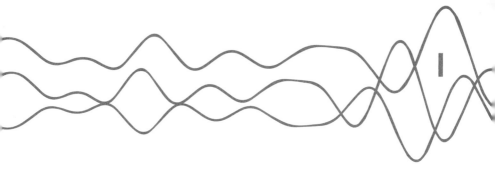

THE HUMAN BODY IS AMAZING," SAYS FRANK EINSTEIN, TO WATSON, in the visitors' dugout of the Midville baseball diamond, watching Janegoodall on the pitcher's mound.

Frank thumbs the joystick on the remote control for his mini FrankenDrone. The little quadcopter swoops into position above the mound and starts beaming pictures back to Frank's display.

Janegoodall turns sideways to home plate.

"There is the whole system of bones making up the skeleton," marvels Frank.

She folds her arms close to her chest, lifting her left leg in a windup.

"The whole muscular system moving the bones . . . ," Frank continues.

Janegoodall strides forward.

"The digestive system producing energy for the muscles . . ."

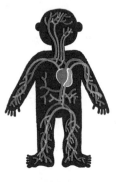

She pushes off the mound with her right leg.

"The heart and blood circulatory system delivering that energy . . ."

Unfolding her arms, turning her body, extending and windmilling her right arm.

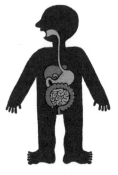

"And the nervous system controlling everything . . . Amazing."

Releasing the baseball from her right hand.

"Mmm-hmm," agrees Watson, thoughtfully sucking a sour lemon candy.

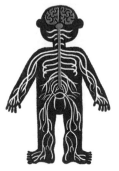

The ball flies from the tips of Janegoodall's fingers and across the forty-six feet to home plate in just over half a second.

Klank swings his bat and misses.

Poom! The ball hits Klink's catcher's mitt.

"Strike one," announces Klink. "Projectile speed, fifty-five miles per hour."

Frank studies the drone pictures and the diagrams of the human body systems on his laptop display. "So all we have to do to help Janegoodall is come up with an invention to make the human body just a bit *more* amazing."

Watson follows his sour lemon with a sweet cherry candy. "That's all? Oh, simple! Just make the human body better than it already is . . . the day before tryouts! Are you crazy?"

"Of course not," says Frank Einstein, bringing the FrankenDrone into the dugout for a perfect landing. "I have some ideas I've already been working on."

Watson pops a hot-cinnamon ball into his mouth. "That's like me saying I'm going to invent a candy that tastes more like candy than it already does."

"Exactly," says Frank.

Klink shoots the baseball back to Janegoodall with his mechanical arm. "Your projectile speed is not bad . . . for a human."

Janegoodall catches the ball, ignores Klink's wisecrack, and walks around the pitcher's mound, giving herself a pep talk. "But I must be faster for the tryouts."

"Put one over the plate," beeps Klank at bat. **"I almost had that one!"**

Klink rolls his webcam eye. "You were not even close."

Frank outlines his thoughts in his human-body lab notebook:

OBSERVATION: *Pitching uses many systems of the human body.*

Janegoodall winds up.

HYPOTHESIS: *Improve even one system, improve pitching results.*

Janegoodall throws.

Klank swings a mighty arc.

Pooom!

"Strike two. Fifty-six miles per hour," says catcher Klink, tossing the ball back to the pitcher's mound.

EXPERIMENT: *Find way to improve skeleton, muscles, digestion, circulation . . . ?*

Watson pops a sunflower seed into his mouth. "I should invent a candy that has all the tastes—sour, sweet, salty . . ."

Frank nudges the remote joystick to relaunch the FrankenDrone. "That might actually be a good idea, Watson."

Janegoodall winds up and throws.

"Hmmm," says Watson. "I could call my candy EveryTaste."

Klank closes his eyes and swings so hard, he spins around like a giant top.

Craaack!

The baseball hits the bat and rockets off. It arches high, higher, up over the left-field wall . . .

Klank twirls. **"I hit it! I hit it! I hit it!"**

"Hardly possible," calculates Klink. "But yes, you did, somehow, hit it."

The ball disappears completely out of Midville Menlo Park.

"Wow," says Frank.

Tsssssssh! There is a sound of breaking glass—from right where the ball disappeared.

"Uh-oh," says Watson, jumping to his feet.

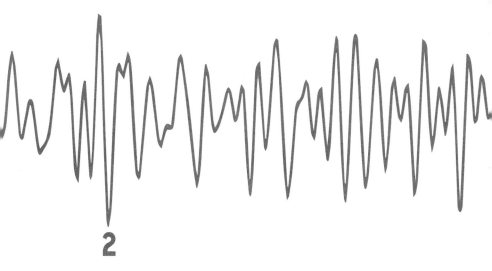

2

THE HUMAN BODY IS WEAK," SAYS T. EDISON, TO MR. CHIMP, IN THE middle of his fancy new T. Edison Laboratories building on Menlo Street, connecting the final electrical power wire to the stem of an enormous glass brain.

Mr. Chimp looks up from his crossword puzzle and nods in agreement.

T. Edison connects the wire. "Human body parts wear out, fall apart, and die."

Mr. Chimp taps his pencil.

"So you know what I am doing?" asks T. Edison.

Mr. Chimp taps his pencil again and pretends he is thinking. He rolls his eyes, shakes his head, and signs:

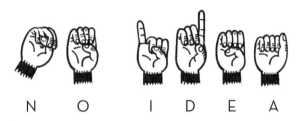

N   O   I   D   E   A

"Of course you have no idea. Because I am the genius inventor and I have all the ideas."

T. Edison turns his invention a bit to set it firmly in its base. "I am making a brain that is faster, more powerful, and better than any *human* brain."

T. Edison flips the power switch. The glass brain glows with lines and pulses of colored light.

"I am making a brain that will not weaken or fall apart. A brain that will allow me to control *other* brains . . ."

T. Edison spreads his arms out and yells in his squeaky voice. "I give you—the T. Edison SuperBrain!"

T. Edison and Mr. Chimp watch the SuperBrain flash with lights, tracing the workings of every part of the brain.

"Yes!" crows T. Edison. "I am the Wizard of Mid—"

Tsssssssh! A section of the glass roof shatters into a

hundred pieces. A shower of glass and one scuffed-up baseball rains down into the room.

The baseball hits the T. Edison SuperBrain.

The SuperBrain explodes in a starburst of colored sparks and wires and broken brain glass.

"Noooooooooooooo!" yells T. Edison. "My SuperBrain! My SuperBrain is destroyed! Who did this?"

Mr. Chimp holds up the baseball as an obvious clue.

T. Edison stomps around in circles, raging. "Who? Who? Who?"

Mr. Chimp ponders a six-letter word for "very intelligent." He tosses the baseball from hand to hand.

T. Edison's brain works out loud. And he finally gets it. "Baseball . . . baseball diamond . . . that's it!" yells T. Edison. "Come on, Mr. Chimp! We're going to the Midville baseball diamond to catch the idiot who wrecked my invention!"

Mr. Chimp fills in 7-Down on his crossword puzzle with G-E-N-I-U-S, then follows the still-fuming T. Edison out the laboratory door.

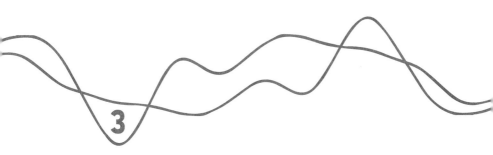

KLINK, KLANK, FRANK, WATSON, AND JANEGOODALL WHEEL, CLOMP, run as fast as they can down Main Street, left on Oak Street, right on Pine, and into Frank Einstein's laboratory. They slam the door shut behind them and fall on the old couch. Frank and Watson and Janegoodall laugh and pant for breath.

Klink and Klank observe their human pals, puzzled.

"What is with the rapid air intake?" asks Klink.

"We used up a lot of oxygen running so fast," explains Frank. "So our bodies are working faster than usual to replace it."

"I see," says Klink, scanning his instant research on the human respiratory system.

"Your muscles are pulling down your diaphragm, causing your lungs to expand, drawing air into your nose and mouth, down your trachea, through your bronchial tubes . . ."

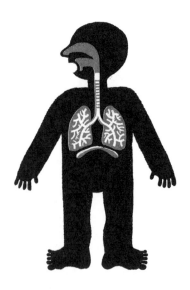

"Exactly," says Frank, parking the FrankenDrone on a shelf above the workbench.

". . . into smaller airways called bronchioles," continues Klink, "that end in small balloon-like air sacs called alveoli, that are surrounded by the smallest blood vessels, called capillaries . . .

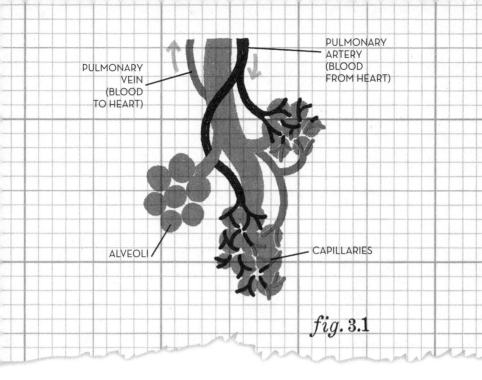

PULMONARY
VEIN
(BLOOD
TO HEART)

PULMONARY
ARTERY
(BLOOD
FROM HEART)

ALVEOLI

CAPILLARIES

fig. 3.1

". . . where the inhaled air passes into the blood and back to the heart, delivering oxygen to the cells and tissues and organs of your body."

"Wow," says Janegoodall.

"No kidding," adds Watson. "Or you could have just said we are out of breath."

"I am not kidding," says Klink. "And why are you laughing?"

This makes Watson and Janegoodall laugh harder.

"We just got away from someone with a broken window who was going to be *very* mad," says Watson.

"Why is that funny?" asks Klink.

"I know why," says Klank. "It is funny like: Why did the chicken cross the road?"

Klink blinks a green light and hums. "From the information you have given me, I cannot tell. Why did the chicken cross the road?"

"To get to the other side!" beeps Klank. "Ha-ha-ha!"

Klink blinks rapidly now.

"What? And why is that funny? Why is it a chicken? What does a chicken . . ."

Klink's hard-drive brain spins and stops, spins and stops.

Frank jumps up and knocks Klink on the side of his glass dome. "Forget the chicken. Time to get going on our experiment."

Frank digs through a pile of broken toys and a heap of brightly colored models. "It's perfect that Grampa Al cleaned out both the old toy store and the old hospital. And added all these great pieces to his Fix It! junkyard."

Frank holds up a giant wind-up cockroach and an over-size model of the human ear. "We've got everything we could possibly need."

"No kidding!" says Watson.

Janegoodall picks up a stuffed dog with no ears and a blue-veined model of a red human heart. "Really? And why exactly do we need all this junk?"

"Here's why," says Frank. "My first idea."

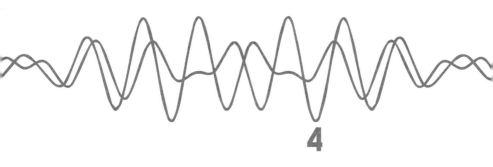

4

FRANK OPENS A TALL LAB CABINET AND WHEELS OUT A FULL-SIZE skeleton.

"Whoa!" says Watson.

"Nice," says Janegoodall.

"Two hundred and six bones total in an adult human being," says Frank. "And you use almost all of them when you pitch."

Janegoodall bends the connected humerus, radius, and ulna arm bones at the elbow joint and then nods.

"I was reading about one of Watson's favorite inventors . . ." Frank pins a picture of an old guy with crazy eyebrows and a long, wavy beard up on the Wall of Science.

Watson licks two of his candies. "Leonardo da Vinci."

Watson sticks the sweet and sour candies together. "Hey! That's an even better name than EveryTaste. I'll call my new candy invention the da Vinci!"

"Born April 15, 1452," Klink recites. "Italian painter, sculptor, inventor, musician, mathematician, engineer, and writer."

"I saw this drawing da Vinci did when he was studying the human body," continues Frank. "And I had the idea—double the skeleton, double the power!"

Janegoodall flips the skeleton's femur. "What?"

"So Klink and Klank and I have an idea for a great improvement." Frank digs around in the pile of toys and models in the lab.

Frank finds what he is searching for and holds up two arms and two legs.

"Wow," says Janegoodall.

Frank and Klink quickly attach the extra arms and legs to Klank.

"Oh yeah!" says Klank. **"Two times arms and two times legs make me two times human!"**

"Ummm, I don't think it works like that," says Janegoodall. "And also—"

"Arms all set!" calls Frank.

"Legs all set," calls Klink.

"Klank all set," calls Klank.

Frank plops a baseball into one of Klank's four hands. "Watson! Come here. I want you . . . to catch. Klink, you record speeds."

Watson puts down his candy invention and picks up the catcher's mitt.

Klank flexes all his arms. **"I am Two Times New, Improved Klank!"**

"Wonderful," says Klink. "It is just a shame that your brain size could not be improved."

"Hey," says Klank. **"Is that a joke?"**

"Test One!" says Frank. "Klank, wind up and pitch a slow ball to Watson."

Klank bends all four of his arms in a double imitation of Janegoodall's windup motion. He steps forward with his two left legs, windmills his two right arms, and pitches a perfect toss to Watson.

"Great," says Frank. "Now back up, really put all four of your arms into it, and try to pitch a little faster."

"Wait, wait, wait a minute," says Watson. "I need some protection." Watson digs through a pile of junk. "Hey, how about a catcher's mask?"

Frank punches out the bottom of a birdcage and hands it to Watson.

"Awww, come on."

"It's for Science," says Frank. "And to help Janegoodall win the starting pitcher spot as our Midville Mud Hen ace."

Watson frowns, but he puts the birdcage on his head and latches the swinging door closed. He pounds the catcher's mitt pocket. "OK. For Science. And for Janegoodall. Come on, bring the heat, Klank."

Klank winds up again. He pitches.

Pooooom!

"Ouch," says Watson.

"Fifty-five miles per hour," reports Klink.

"A little faster," Frank directs.

Klank winds up. And pitches.

Pooooom!

"Yowwwww!" yells Watson.

"Sixty-five miles per hour."

"Full speed!" Frank calls.

Klank winds up. Klank fires.

Pooooom!

"Seventy-five miles per hour."

"Yikes!" says Watson. "But also . . . oops."

"Brilliant," says Janegoodall. "Just brilliant. But not so brilliant when Klank's hand went seventy-five miles per hour along *with* the ball."

Frank Einstein checks Klank's handless arm and shakes his head.

"And," adds Janegoodall, "there is no way you are sticking any extra arms or legs on me."

5

T. EDISON CHARGES INTO MIDVILLE MENLO BASEBALL PARK.

"All right! Who knocked this baseball into my lab, broke my roof, *and* wrecked my experiment?!"

Mr. Chimp looks around the baseball diamond and sniffs.

No one answers T. Edison because there is no one there.

T. Edison walks around the pitcher's mound. "Fresh marks in the dirt," he observes. "Someone was just here."

Mr. Chimp knuckle-walks his way into the visitors' dugout. He picks up a sunflower seed. He looks at it. He pinches it. He smells it. He pops it in his mouth.

"Mmmmm," says Mr. Chimp, tasting the salt.

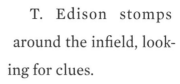

T. Edison stomps around the infield, looking for clues.

Mr. Chimp cracks the sunflower seed between his top and bottom premolars. He spits out the empty sunflower shell with a satisfying *p-tuuu* sound.

T. Edison crawls around home plate on his hands and knees. He holds a dirt-covered piece of bubble gum up in the light.

"Aha! I can isolate the saliva from this gum, extract the DNA, match it to the DNA of everyone in Midville, and identify the glass-breaker!"

Mr. Chimp leans back on the visitors' bench. He picks up another sunflower seed, pops it in his mouth, and shakes his head.

"What?" fumes T. Edison. "Yes, I can! Every living organism has DNA. It is a molecule that carries the instructions for how every organism is formed. It is what every organism uses to reproduce."

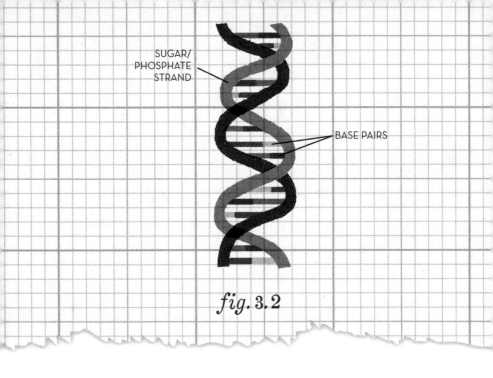

SUGAR/
PHOSPHATE
STRAND

BASE PAIRS

fig. 3.2

Mr. Chimp cracks the sunflower seed, this time using his incisors, and signs:

I   K   N   O   W

T. Edison smacks his forehead and rants some more. "And as much as I hate to admit it, ninety-eight percent of human DNA is the same as chimpanzee DNA."

Mr. Chimp nods.

I   K   N   O   W

T. Edison shakes the dirty gum at Mr. Chimp. "Stop saying that! If you know so much, why don't you explain how we catch the vandals who wrecked my invention?"

Mr. Chimp spits out the empty shell with another satisfying *p-tuuu*. He holds up a worn brown baseball glove he found under the bench. He turns the glove around to show T. Edison the name written on the

back in big black letters:

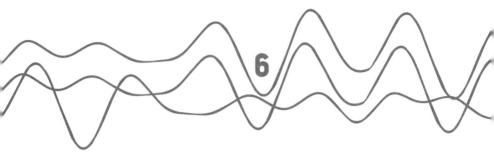

6

FRANK EINSTEIN TIGHTENS THE LAST BOLT ON KLANK'S TWO ORIGINAL arms. Klink oils Klank's two original legs.

Klank sighs. **"I liked my new arms and legs."**

"OK," says Frank, "so the new and improved skeletal system didn't work out. But how about this?"

Frank pulls out a big canvas poster, unrolls it, and pins it on the Wall of Science.

"The muscular system. Humans have over six hundred and fifty muscles. Some automatic—like our heart and breathing muscles. Others controlled by thoughts, for movement."

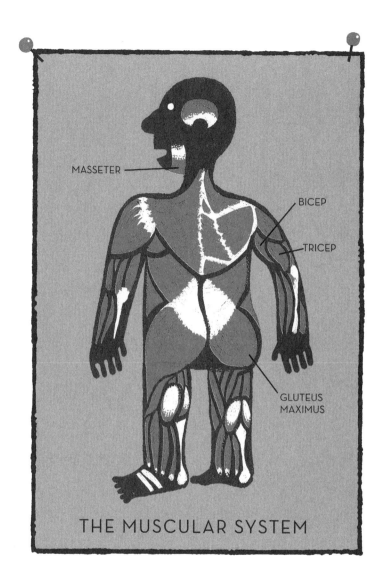

MASSETER

BICEP

TRICEP

GLUTEUS
MAXIMUS

THE MUSCULAR SYSTEM

Klink hums and offers his latest research. "The stron-
gest human muscle is the masseter. It moves the jaw.
And the biggest human muscle is the gluteus maximus.

It keeps the human body upright. Also powers running and jumping. This is your butt muscle."

"Ha-ha-ha!" beeps Klank.

"Now what is so funny?" asks Klink.

"You said butt muscle! Ha-ha-ha!"

Klink checks his research. **"Yes, that is correct. The gluteus maximus is also called the butt. And it is a muscle."**

Klank falls on the couch laughing. **"Ha-ha-ha!"**

"Oooooooooo," hums Klink.

Frank ignores Klink and Klank. Thinking out loud, he says, "Muscles are attached to bones by tendons. A lot of muscles work in pairs. Like in Janegoodall's arm. To bend the arm, the bicep tightens and the tricep relaxes. To straighten the arm, the tricep tightens and the bicep relaxes."

"So bigger and stronger muscles could also pitch the ball faster," figures Watson.

Janegoodall studies the muscular system chart. "Again, brilliant . . . except for the fact that we have exactly one day before the tryouts. And I don't have time to lift weights to make my muscles bigger."

"I've got it!" says Watson. "We switch your small bicep . . . with your large gluteus maximus . . . for a Super-Power Butt-Muscle Arm!"

"Ha-ha-ha!" Klank giggles again.

Janegoodall whacks both Watson and Klank with her Midville Mud Hens hat. "Very funny. But we need a real idea for more power. Like—right now!"

"OK," says Frank Einstein. "Back to the drawing board."

7

THE PANZER TANK ROLLS OVER A SMALL ARMY OF NEON-GREEN jittering bugs and pushes the purple monster truck into the corner of the lab.

"I've got you now!" hoots Watson. "Demolition Derby!"

"You wish," says Klank. He turns his monster truck wheels, hits full power, and escapes by rolling his big tires right over the top of Watson's tank.

Frank scratches his head with one hand and checks the math on his blueprint with the other.

Watson jams his tank into fast reverse. He tries to slam Klank's truck but misses and smashes a rainbow-hearted pony.

"*Raaahhhhhr!*" roars a one-legged T. Rex.

"*Wee tah kah loo-loo,*" moans a one-eyed purple Furby, wriggling on its back.

Klank spins his monster truck around to face Watson's tank.

Watson turns the Panzer turret to aim its cannon right at Klank's truck.

"Come on, you guys," says Frank. "We need your help."

Watson and Klank count down together: "Three . . . two . . . one!" and forward-charge each other. The monster truck plows over the T. Rex. The tank plows through the Furby. And all four—truck, T. Rex, tank, and Furby—crash in one giant pileup and land in a motionless heap.

"Yeah!" cheers Watson.

"Who wins?" asks Klank.

From somewhere under the toy wreck pile, the Furby says, "*Doo doo yoo yoo,*" and with a *bzzzzzzt*, shorts out.

Frank Einstein digs through a pile of medical charts and models and posters.

He chews the eraser end of his pencil. He scratches his head. He thinks. He unrolls a poster. "OK—here's another system we could boost for more power."

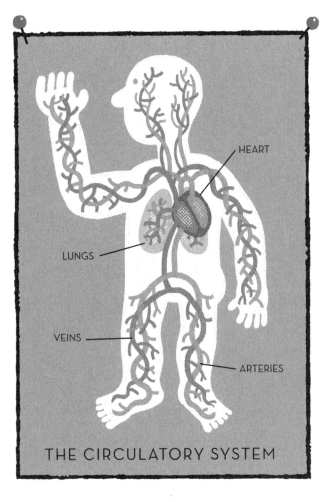

THE CIRCULATORY SYSTEM

"The circulatory system. The heart and all the blood vessels that deliver energy and oxygen to the muscles and organs," reports Klink, after instantly reading a whole stack of medical encyclopedias in exactly three seconds. "Blood is pumped away from the heart in arteries. Blood is returned to the heart in veins."

With his chewed pencil, Frank traces the path of blood in a heart-lung diagram.

"The heart pumps blood to the lungs. That blood picks up oxygen and goes back to the heart, then out to the rest of the body."

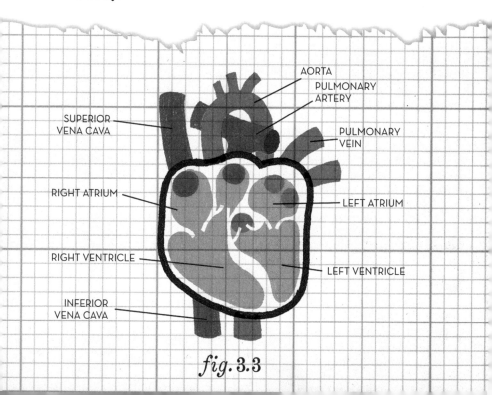

fig. **3.3**

Janegoodall drops her hat on the lab table. She looks at the heart diagram and gives a whistle. "Woowwww. The heart is a crazy, complicated thing!"

"The human heart is about the size of two hands held together. It beats one hundred thousand times a day. It pumps one and a half gallons of blood every minute. The heartbeat is the sound of valves opening and closing," adds Klink.

"And check out these great crazy names," says Watson.

Frank traces more on a 3D heart model:

"Blood flows through the *superior vena cava* into the *right atrium*. It's pumped to the *right ventricle* and flows out to the lungs through the *pulmonary artery*. It flows back from the lungs through the *pulmonary vein* into the *left atrium*. It's then pumped to the *left ventricle* and out to the body through the *aorta*. Simple."

Watson fiddles with his growing candy-ball invention. "I don't think I'd call that *simple*. And how the heck do we boost this? Or the blood system?"

"Like this," says Frank. "The blood carries oxygen to the muscles for more power. If we can figure out a way for the blood to carry more *oxygen* . . . we can produce more *power*."

"Without giving me any extra arms or messing with my gluteus maximus," adds Janegoodall.

"Exactly," says Frank.

Watson shakes his head and reaches in his pocket for a sunflower seed to add to his invention. "Oh no!" says Watson.

"Oh yes," answers Frank. "See, the red blood cells absorb oxygen—"

Watson looks suddenly a bit panicked. "I mean—oh no, I forgot my sunflower seeds back at the baseball diamond."

"This is not the time to worry about sunflower seeds, Watson."

"Uhhhhh, but I think I forgot my sunflower seeds *and* my baseball glove . . . with my name written on it."

"Why does that matter?" asks Frank.

The answer to that question comes as a sudden pounding on Frank Einstein's laboratory door.

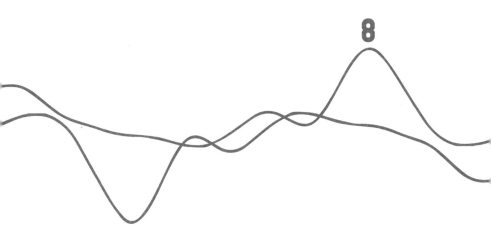

8

BAM! BAM! BAM!

The whole door of Frank Einstein's laboratory shakes.

Bam! Bam! Bam!

It sounds like someone with the strength of three men is pounding on the door.

Bam! Bam! Bam!

Frank checks his spy cam.

Bam! Bam! Bam!

It *is* someone with the strength of three men.

"Mr. Chimp!"

"Open up," calls a squirrelly voice.

Frank recognizes the voice. "And T. Edison, too! What could they want?"

"Nothing good, I'm sure," whispers Watson. He ducks behind the workbench. "Let's pretend we're not here."

"And don't pretend you're not there!" yells T. Edison. "I know you're in there. Mr. Chimp can smell you."

Frank opens his laboratory door.

T. Edison, looking even goofier than usual because he is wearing orange high-top tennis shoes, steps into Frank Einstein's laboratory with his hands behind his back.

Mr. Chimp, his assistant and chief financial officer, slides in behind him. He stands with his back to the wall.

"Well, hello, Yogi and Boo Boo," says T. Edison. "So nice to see you . . . again."

"So unfortunate to see you and your ape . . . again," says Frank.

Edison looks around the lab, eyeballing the Wall of Science, the diagrams and models and posters on the lab table, and the pile of electronic parts and toys on the floor.

"And hello, Janegoodall. What are you doing hanging out with these losers?"

Janegoodall doesn't answer. She just gives Edison a small nod, because she is much more fascinated by the real, live version of her favorite subject—primates—standing by the door.

Watson can't stand it. "What are *you* doing here, Edison? You are *always* bad news."

"Me? Bad news?" says Edison in fake surprise. "Good heavens, no. I'm just a fellow scientist."

"Who took the Antimatter Motor," says Klink.

"Who tried to destroy the Electro-Finger," adds Klank.

"Oh, look!" says T. Edison to Mr. Chimp. "It's Frank Einstein's talking vacuum cleaner and walking trash can friends—Plink and Plunk."

"That is wrong," says Klank. **"My name is Klank. And Klink's name is . . . Klink."**

Frank flips over his invention sketches on the table. "What do you want, Edison?"

"Oh, I don't *want* anything. I came to give you something."

Mr. Chimp rocks from one foot to the other and gives a little cough.

"Yeah right," says Watson.

T. Edison smiles. Or at least he tries to. It comes out looking more like a show of teeth.

From behind his back, Edison pulls out a baseball glove and flips it around to show the name written on it. "Watson, I presume?"

"Hey! There is your baseball glove!" booms Klank.

"Thanks, Klank. I can see that," says a red-faced Watson.

"But why do you have it?" asks Frank.

T. Edison tosses the glove to Watson. "Oh, Mr. Chimp and I just happened to find it in Midville Menlo Park . . . after *this* came through my very expensive new laboratory roof and crashed into my most amazing invention!"

T. Edison holds out his other hand.

Mr. Chimp nods and hooo-hoots.

"Hey!" booms Klank again.

Watson tries to cover up Klank's mouth speaker but can't quite reach him in time.

"And that is our baseball!"

Mr. Chimp claps his leathery hands and signs:

B U S T E D

Edison walks around the lab like he owns it now. He plops the baseball on Frank's workbench.

"Yes, this is your baseball. It broke my glass roof. It ruined my invention. So now you must pay for everything."

"But we don't have any money," Watson protests.

T. Edison runs a finger over the human-heart model. "Oh, that is so sad. I guess you will have to work for me, then." Edison picks up a brain model. "Or give me one of your inventions as payment."

Frank takes the brain model away from T. Edison. "Not likely."

Frank and T. Edison stand nose to nose, eye to eye.

The lab is dead quiet.

Then Mr. Chimp knocks over a metal trash can with a sudden *clang-crash!* He grabs a broomstick and drags it behind him, hops around the lab, sweeps tools and books

off tables, knocks down shelves, hoot-screams as he flips over cans and boxes and anything in his path.

Frank and Watson jump back in shock. Klink and Klank get out of Mr. Chimp's way. No one knows quite what to do.

Except Janegoodall. She stays exactly where she is and doesn't move a muscle.

Mr. Chimp hops and hoots and slaps the table right next to Janegoodall.

She still doesn't move.

Mr. Chimp pauses. He turns his head to look at Janegoodall, then charges—slapping and screaming— right out the door.

T. Edison tilts his head, follows, stops, and turns.

"Like Mr. Chimp says: Pay up . . . or else."

T. Edison leaves and slams the lab door shut behind him.

Watson peeks out from behind the workbench. "Geez! That is one crazy monkey!"

"Ape," Janegoodall corrects Watson. "And not really crazy. That was a very deliberate territory and dominance display."

"A wha—?" says Watson.

"A demonstration to tell us that he is in charge of Midville, and that he is in charge of us," says Frank.

9

slings her gear bag over her shoulder. "OK, geniuses. I'm outta here. I've got to keep practicing. You let me know if you come up with anything."

Frank carefully places the brain model back on the shelf. "We will. We always do."

"See you laters, alligators," calls Janegoodall on her way out the door.

Watson sets the trash can back upright.

Klank picks up the baseball. **"Very good. We have our baseball. Watson has his glove."**

"No," says Watson. "This is not so very good. We don't have enough money to pay off Edison. And we don't—"

Brrrrrrrnnnnngggg ahhhhchooo! The oversize model of the human nose suddenly ring-sneezes.

"*Yahhhhhh!*" yells Watson, jumping to his feet.

Brrrrrrrnnnnngggg ahhhhchooo! The nose ring-sneezes again.

"Why is that nose ringing?" asks Watson.

"Grampa Al rewired the phone again," explains Frank. He picks up an equally oversize model of the human ear and answers into it, "Hello, Einstein Laboratories."

"Hello, sweetie," says the nose.

"Oh, hi, Mom."

"How are you and Grampa Al doing? Are you staying out of trouble?"

Frank looks around the trashed lab.

"Um . . . yeah! Mostly. Just getting ready for the Midville Mud

Hens tryouts tomorrow. And Watson is over. We're working on some . . . uh . . . human-body inventions."

"We are throwing a baseball very fast," adds Klank.

"Attempting to throw," corrects Klink.

"Oh, hello, Klink and Klank. What's new with my favorite robots?"

"In the two minutes since you called, I have scanned eight hundred and seventy-two new books. I have also added seven hundred ten thousand one hundred and forty-four new connections in my electronic brain," answers Klink.

"Oh my!" says Mom Einstein.

"I am reading *Go, Dog. Go!* **by P. D. Eastman,"** says Klank. **"The green dog is up. And the yellow dog is down. And T. Edison came to visit with his assistant, Mr. Chimp, and they—"**

"Are all doing just great!" says Frank, cutting off Klank. "How are you and Dad?"

"We have found the most wonderful spots to tour," says Mom Einstein through the NosePhone. "The Franklin Institute here is fascinating. Did you know that Benjamin

Franklin invented bifocals and swim fins?"

"Oh, he's another one of my favorite inventors," says Watson. "Maybe my candy invention should be called the Franklin."

"Frank, your father wants to tell you something."

"Helloooooooo from the Keystone State!" booms the NosePhone.

"Hi, Dad."

"The City of Brotherly Love!"

"Philadelphia, right?" says Frank.

"Home of Independence Hall, the Liberty Bell, the cheesesteak, and cream cheese, I believe. Can you guess where we are?"

"Benjamin Franklin invented the cheesesteak?" asks Klank.

Klink instantly checks his memory banks. "No."

"Hello, Klank," says Dad Einstein. "That reminds me of a great Philadelphia joke. Did you hear the one about the Liberty Bell?"

"No," beeps Klank.

"It will crack you up!"

"Ha-ha-ha!"

"What is the joke?" asks Klink.

"That *is* the joke."

"What is?"

"That is!"

"Rrrrrrrrrrrrr bzzzzt bzzzzzt bzzzzt." Klink shorts out.

"There are all kinds of great science museums here," says Dad through the NosePhone. "But right now we are in the craziest place I have ever seen—the Mütter Museum. It's a whole collection of models of the human body, real bones, and real preserved body parts."

"Whoa!" says Frank. "That sounds amazing."

"A collection of one hundred and eighty-nine skulls," Dad Einstein continues, "and one doctor's collection of two thousand three hundred and seventy-four weird things that people swallowed or inhaled!"

"Gross!" says Watson.

"Fantastic!" says Frank.

"And the most amazing thing of all—the museum has pieces of Albert Einstein's brain!"

"What? Are you kidding?"

"I am not kidding. Ohhh, but we have to run. One more spot to check out for travelallovertheplace.com—the Pizza Museum!"

Mom Einstein chimes in. "Bye, sweetie. We'll be home on Tuesday. Don't forget to brush your teeth."

Frank hangs up the ear.

"A pizza museum!" marvels Watson. "Now *that's* genius."

"Liberty Bell joke," beeps Klank. **"It will crack you up."**

"Rrrrrrrrrr." Klink spins, still trying to compute what was funny.

"Einstein's brain?" wonders Frank. "Einstein... brain...?"

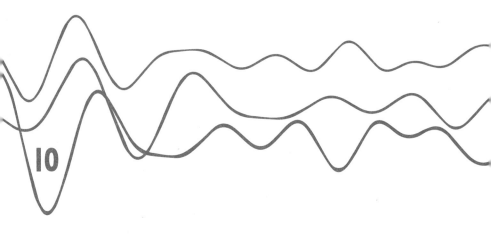

10

TEDISON AND MR. CHIMP SIT ON THE PLUSH RUG IN THE WARM, sunlit glass tower of the new T. Edison Laboratories. They are surrounded by talking dolls, talking tigers, talking parrots, talking reindeer, alligators, sheep, bears, cowboys, spacemen, princesses, chickens, pickles, mermaids, pigs, frogs, cars, elephants, hamsters, babies, aliens, gorillas, and a talking toilet.

Mr. Chimp smacks his lips, enjoying his favorite breakroom snack—the T. Edison PowerMix of figs, nuts, and termites.

T. Edison loudly slurps the last of his apple juice box and picks up a blue-eyed, blonde-pigtailed doll. He gives her a squeeze.

"*Twinkle, twinkle, little star,*" sings the smiling doll, "*how I wonder what you are.*"

"Hmm," grunts Mr. Chimp.

T. Edison twists off her head and pulls out the voice mechanism.

"This is what I'm talking about, Mr. Chimp. Inventions are the thing—we stay on schedule, one small invention every ten days, one big invention every six months."

Mr. Chimp picks up a gorilla and an alien. He presses their voice buttons and makes them talk to each other.

"*Oook oook.*"

"Take me to your leader."

T. Edison examines the doll's insides with his magnifying glass. "Inventions are good. We register everything we make. But the real game is in selling products! Making money!"

Mr. Chimp smashes the alien and gorilla together, knocking off both their heads. And enjoying it.

T. Edison walks over to the circle of windows that makes up the huge glass-topped tower of T. Edison Laboratories. He looks out over the panorama of eastside Midville far below.

"Look at all those little human minds down there, just waiting to be told what to do, what to think, what to *buy*!"

Edison looks through a pair of polished brass-and-aluminum 20 mm x 120 mm Japanese World War II battleship binoculars. The powerful lenses, working like a super-version of an eye, magnify scenes from miles around.

"There's Police Sergeant Susan, saving a kitten. Postman Charlie, delivering a package. Fireman Chad, fixing his firehose. And Police Chief and Head Coach Jacobs right there in Midville Menlo Park, raking the mound for tomorrow's Mud Hens Team tryouts.

"What a bunch of saps! They will be the perfect victims—
I mean, customers—when we rebuild my T. Edison
SuperBrain . . . and make them do whatever I want."

Mr. Chimp pulls a leg off a mechanical frog.

"Now let's get to work. Because you know what I always
say."

Mr. Chimp signs:

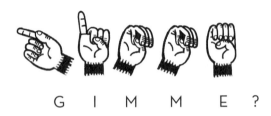

"Don't be a wise guy," says Edison, tossing the headless
doll body on the toy pile. "Like that other Edison, I always
say, 'Invention is one percent inspiration and ninety-nine
percent perspiration.'"

"Yes, really! And that's why people call me the Wizard of Midville."

Mr. Chimp tries everything he can to say the words "They do?" But his chimpanzee voice box is just not built for speech.

The best he can do is a short *"Hrrrrrrr?"*

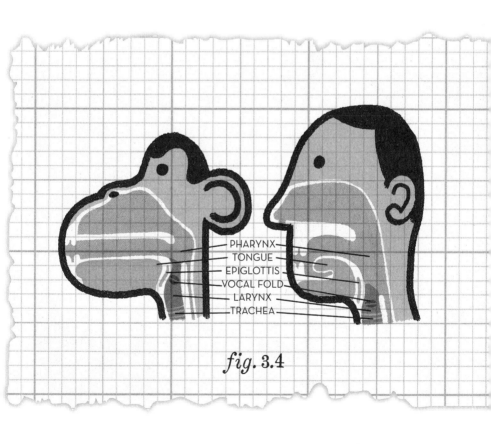

PHARYNX
TONGUE
EPIGLOTTIS
VOCAL FOLD
LARYNX
TRACHEA

fig. 3.4

"Absolutely," replies Grampa Al from under his Fix It! shop truck.

"How come you never told me?"

"You never asked."

Grampa Al rolls his mechanic's creeper under the front of the truck and holds out an open palm like a brain surgeon. "Flex-head . . . uh . . . doohickey."

"Flex-head ratchet?" asks Frank.

"Oh . . . yeah. That's what I meant. Good golly, this turbo-charger is going to boost this engine faster than a sneeze through a screen door."

"How will it do that?" asks Watson, sitting on the shop floor to get a closer look at both the tools and turbocharger.

"It's a turbine that pushes more air into the engine's combustion chamber . . . that burns more fuel . . . that makes more power."

Frank wheels his chair over to Grampa Al's toolbox. He picks out the adjustable ratchet, wheels back, and slaps the tool in Grampa Al's hand.

"Wait, wait—back to Einstein's brain. How could that ever get lost? He was one of the most genius and famous scientists ever."

"Wellll . . ." Grampa Al tightens a bolt. "That's an interesting question. Historians are pretty sure Einstein didn't want anybody messing around with his brain, making a big deal of it."

Grampa Al tightens one more bolt with a quick bunch of ratcheting clicks, then rolls out from under his truck. He pops up the hood, leans in, and opens his palm again. "Flat-head . . . you know . . . whatchamacallit . . ."

"Screwdriver?" says Frank.

"Yeah. Sheesh. Forgetting the name of everything these days."

Frank hands over the big flat-head screwdriver. Grampa Al tightens the last hose clamp, rechecks his connections, and refills the truck engine with oil.

"But the guy at the hospital who conducted the autopsy, dissecting the body to study disease—uhhh . . . the pathologist, that's what you call him—who was on duty the day Einstein died, took the brain without asking anybody."

"But you can't do that, can you?" says Watson.

"Thomas Harvey did," says Grampa Al. He empties the last oil can and tightens the oil cap. "A couple days later, he got permission from Einstein's son, Hans. And the deal was that any study of the brain would be done strictly for science. Not for making money or making Einstein more famous."

"That sounds reasonable," says Frank. "And it would be a good way to see what made Einstein so smart, right? Seeing if there were parts of his brain that were different?"

Grampa Al wipes his hands on a blue shop rag. He goes over to his computer and scrolls through some files. "You would think so. But this was back in 1955. The technology for anatomy study wasn't very advanced. Harvey hoped maybe the brain could be preserved until better technology was invented. So he took a bunch of pictures. And he measured and preserved the brain the best he could. Hmmm. Oh, here it is."

Grampa Al clicks on a file, and a picture flashes up on the Fix It! garage wall.

"There it is—Einstein's brain."

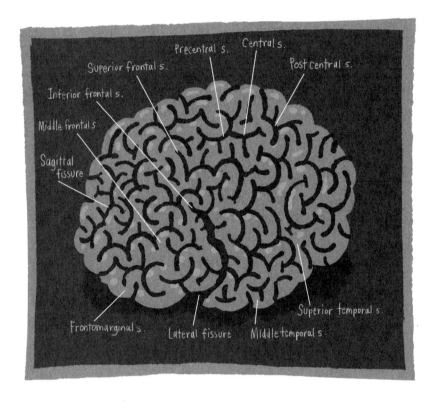

"No way," says Frank. "So what did scientists find out when they studied it?"

"Well, here's where the story goes strange," says Grampa Al. "Harvey didn't get anyone to study the brain. He lost his job at Princeton Hospital. And he took the brain with him. He cut it up into a couple hundred pieces and put them all in preservative in two Mason jars."

"Yuck!" says Watson. "You mean those glass jars my grandma uses for tomatoes?"

"Exactly," says Grampa Al. "And then, over the next twenty years or so, everybody forgot about Einstein's brain. It was in the seventies that I ran into this fella Tom in Wichita, Kansas. And after talking to him for a bit, getting to know him, I come to find out he is Thomas Harvey. And he has Einstein's brain, still in those two Mason jars, in his basement, in a wooden box."

"What?!" says Frank.

Grampa Al fires up the truck engine, checks for leaks, then slams the hood. "Yep."

"What were you doing in Wichita, Kansas?"

Grampa Al squints one eye. "Long story. Remind me to tell you sometime. I gotta run and pick up some more . . . ummm . . . thingamabobs . . ."

"But whatever happened to Einstein's brain? Has anybody studied it? Do we know what made him a genius?"

Grampa Al leans out the truck window. "I connected Harvey with some magazine people. They did a story. Couple of other folks have taken a look at the pieces. But nobody can say for sure."

Watson and Frank stare at the old black-and-white shot on the wall.

"The brain is the most amazing organ," says Grampa Al. "It's the driver of the whole machine that is the human body. It controls everything."

Grampa Al puts the truck in gear, yells, "Turbocharge!" and peels out with a squeal of hot rubber and a cloud of white smoke.

Frank stares at the picture of Einstein's brain. He thinks out loud. "The driver of the whole machine. Controlling everything. Turbocharge."

Frank scratches his head, messing up his hair like he always does when he is thinking.

"Watson, this gives me an idea."

12

YES," SAYS FRANK, LOOKING OVER THE EXPLOSION OF PICTURES, diagrams, notes, and drawings on the Wall of Science. He studies the mess of medical models and broken toys.

"Skeletal system. Muscular system. Circulatory system. Digestive system. Respiratory system. Nervous system. Ben Franklin. Albert Einstein's brain. Turbocharger . . ."

Millions of nerve cells flash and connect in Frank Einstein's brain.

A pattern of connections—an idea—forms.

"OK, team. Let's go. Watson, collect all the remotes. Break them down."

Watson grabs a handful of controllers and starts opening them with his screwdriver. "Will do!"

"Klank, get everything with any kind of electronic brain."

Klank scoops up the one-legged T. Rex and an old toaster.

"Oooooh-kay!"

"Klink, we need info on all the five senses. How they are built. How they work. Can you do that?"

"Done."

"What do you mean, 'done'?"

"As in the usual definition of the word *done*," beeps Klink. "Finished. Completed. Ready for examination."

"Wow," says Frank. "You *are* fast."

"I am Klink. Which sense do you want first?"

Frank scratches his head again. "Sight."

Sight is the perception of light and color and size and shape.

A transparent LENS in the eye directs light onto the RETINA.

The retina is made of cells that detect:

- light
- color

The RETINA CELLS send electrical signals through the OPTIC NERVE to the BRAIN.

The signals from both eyes are combined to create a complete image by the BRAIN.

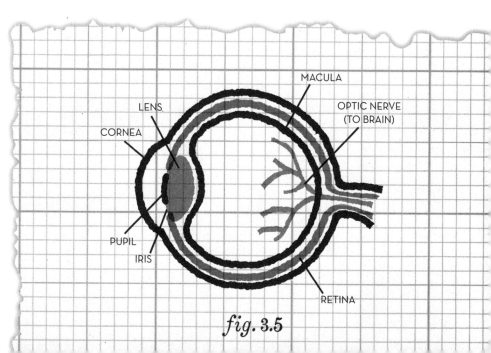

fig. 3.5

It is impossible to sneeze with your eyes open.

Male humans are more likely to be color blind (seeing green and red as gray) than female humans.

EXPERIMENT: YOUR BLIND SPOT

The spot inside your eye where the optic nerve exits your eyeball does not have light receptors. So it is a blind spot in your vision.

BLIND SPOT TESTER

●   +

- Hold this Blind Spot Tester an arm's length away from you.
- Close your right eye.
- Look at the cross with your left eye.
- Move the paper around until the dot disappears.

Congratulations! You found your blind spot.

Now try it the other way:

- Close your left eye.
- Look at the dot with your right eye.
- Move the paper until the cross disappears.

Blind spot!

"Yes!" Frank nods. "This is great stuff."

"What?" beeps Klink. "This is how the sense of sight works. It is not 'stuff.'"

"You know what I mean."

"Hmmm. No, I do not."

Frank draws a line on his invention blueprint. "OK. Never mind."

"Hmmm. How do I 'never mind'?"

"Next sense!"

12.2 HEARING

Hearing is the perception of sound vibrations.

The OUTER EAR directs sound vibrations to the EARDRUM.

The eardrum sends the vibrations through the tiny bones of the MIDDLE EAR.

The middle-ear bones transmit the vibrations to the INNER EAR, to nerve fibers in the HAIR CELLS there that send impulses through the AUDITORY NERVE to the BRAIN.

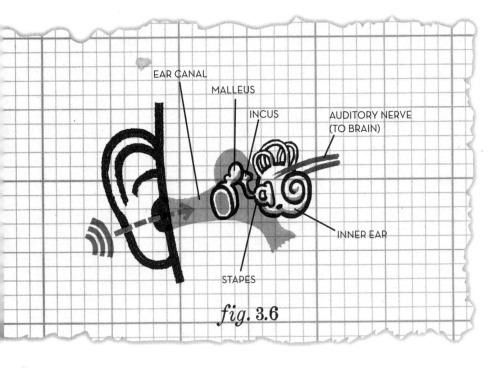

EAR CANAL

MALLEUS

INCUS

AUDITORY NERVE
(TO BRAIN)

INNER EAR

STAPES

fig. 3.6

The stapes is the smallest bone in the human body.

Ears are self-cleaning. Little hairs called cilia push out earwax and dirt.

EXPERIMENT: HEAR LIKE AN ELEPHANT

The outer ear collects sound waves. Do bigger outer ears collect more sound waves?

- Take a big piece of paper and roll it into a cone shape with one end as large as possible, the other end with an opening about as big as a dime. Tape the paper so it doesn't come undone.
- Hold the small end of the cone close to your ear.
- Walk around the room and listen to sounds. You should be able to hear more sounds, and hear quiet sounds more clearly.

"Exactly," says Frank Einstein, sketching another section of his invention blueprint. "Next sense!"

Klink hums.

NERVE CELLS in the skin (and tongue and throat) detect:

- movement
- pressure
- heat
- cold
- pain

Nerve cells send signals through the nervous system to the BRAIN.

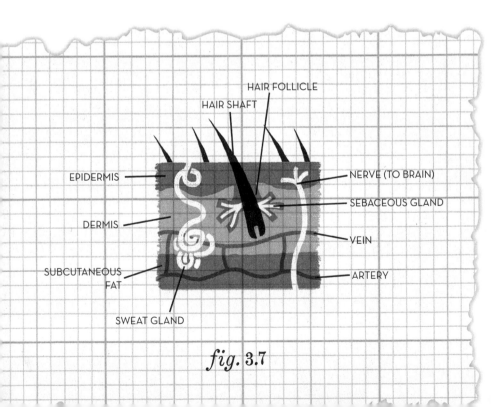

fig. 3.7

The skin is the human body's largest organ.

The color of skin depends on the amount of a pigment called melanin produced by the body. Large amounts of melanin make skin dark. Small amounts of melanin make skin light.

The thickest skin on humans is on the bottom of our feet and the palms of our hands.

Hairy parts of the body are more sensitive because the hairs in the skin magnify feeling.

Some parts of the body, like our fingertips, have a greater concentration of nerve cells than other parts of the body.

Humans lose around fifty million skin cells per day. So most of the dust in your house is dead skin cells.

EXPERIMENT:
WHERE ARE THE MOST NERVE CELLS?

- Get a friend and a large paper clip.
- Straighten the paper clip, then bend it into a U shape.
- Have your friend close their eyes.
- Lightly touch the two ends of the paper clip at the same time to the back of your friend's hand.
- Ask your friend if they feel one or two pressure points. If they feel one, spread the tips farther apart. If they feel two, push the tips closer together.
- Measure the distance between tips when your friend says they feel two points. Write down the distance between points.
- Now try the test on different parts of the body— arm, leg, cheek, back, fingertip. How do the different measurements compare? The closer the points, the more nerve cells.

Frank squints at his sketch and scratches his head. "Fifty million skin cells?"

"Every day," buzzes Klink. "Humans. So untidy."

Frank taps his pencil, lost in thought.

"OK, next!"

12.4 TASTE

Taste is the ability to detect sweet, salty, sour, bitter, or umami (savory) flavors.

The human tongue has an average of ten thousand TASTE BUDS.

Each taste bud is made of roughly one hundred TASTE RECEPTOR CELLS.

The taste receptor cells send signals through the nervous system to the BRAIN.

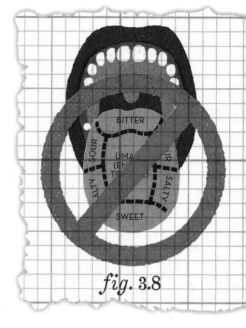

fig. 3.8

The tongue also has receptor cells that detect heat, cold, and texture.

Taste receptor cells die and are replaced every few days.

Female humans have more taste buds than male humans.

EXPERIMENT: BRAIN FREEZE RELIEF

Brain freeze happens when cold food makes contact with the roof of your mouth.

Your nerve cells send signals to your brain that your body is cold.

Your brain sends signals back to make your blood vessels smaller to save heat.

The shrinking blood vessels cause a numbing pain in your head.

So the next time you get brain freeze, you can cure it by telling your brain, as quickly as you can, that you are warm enough. Do that by warming the roof of your mouth.

Try these three ways to see which works best for you:

- Put your thumb in your mouth, and press on the roof of your mouth.
- Flip your tongue up, and push the hot underside of your tongue against the roof of your mouth.
- Cup your hands over your mouth and nose. Breathe in and out to warm the roof of your mouth.

Watson holds up his salted cherry-lemon candy ball and a taste map of the human tongue.

"I *knew* that tongue taste map in our science book was wrong!" says Watson. "I can prove it with this simple experiment. I taste my da Vinci candy with the tip of my tongue . . . and I can taste the salt flavor!"

"The tongue taste map is not correct," adds Klink. "Receptors for all tastes are found throughout the tongue."

Watson looks at the map. "But I do still need to add bitter and umami to the da Vinci."

"That might be too much," says Frank.

Watson taste-tests his invention. "Mmmm, da Vinci. It's da-licious."

"That is seriously too much. Next sense, Klink!"

12.5 SMELL

Smell is the sense of detecting odor through the nose.

Tiny SCENT MOLECULES (from flowers, popcorn, dog poop, everything) float through the air and enter the nose.

The scent molecules trigger RECEPTOR CELLS located high inside the nose.

The receptor cells send signals to the OLFAC-TORY BULB.

The olfactory bulb passes the signals to both the primitive, unconscious part of the BRAIN and the conscious, thinking part of the BRAIN.

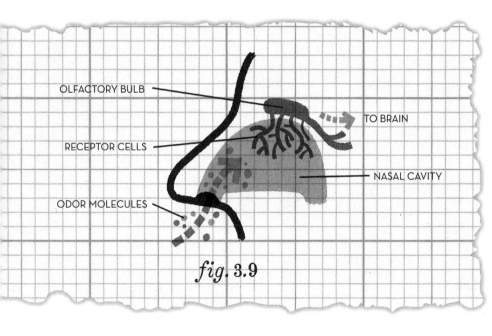

OLFACTORY BULB

TO BRAIN

RECEPTOR CELLS

NASAL CAVITY

ODOR MOLECULES

fig. 3.9

When humans sleep, their sense of smell shuts down.

Female humans have more receptors and a better sense of smell than male humans.

Emotions and memories can be triggered by smell.

EXPERIMENT: CAN YOU TASTE WITHOUT SMELL?

- Cut up a peeled potato and peeled apple into small, equal-size pieces.
- Plug your nose with your fingers.
- Without looking, eat pieces of apple and potato . . . and see if you can tell which is which.

This would explain why it's difficult to taste anything when you have a cold and your nose is stuffed up.

Frank jumps up and paces around the workbench. He rubs his head with both hands, messing up his hair completely wild and crazy. "Yes, yes, yes."

Klink reviews his smell explanation. "What are emotions and memories?"

Frank stops pacing. "Huh?"

"Emotions and memories," repeats Klink. "That can be triggered by smell. What are they?"

"Emotions are . . . feelings. Like being happy, or sad, or mad."

"Right," says Klink. "And what is happy, or sad, or mad?"

Frank explains, "Happy is . . . well . . . feeling good about something."

"Hmmm," hums Klink. "You are not explaining feelings. You are just repeating the same words."

"It's very complicated," says Frank. "Ask Grampa Al."

"OK," beeps Klink. "I will. And one more question."

Frank adds another bit to his invention blueprint. "Yes?"

"Why are female humans different from male humans?"

Frank thinks about that for a long moment.

"You should *definitely* ask Grampa Al about that."

"Here you go!" says Watson.

He plows through the backyard door, pulling a wagon piled with TV, DVD, and garage-door remotes. Xbox, PlayStation, and model-toy controllers. Steering wheels, gaming pads, flight sticks, and switch panels.

Watson dumps the wagonload in a pile on the floor. "And I've got them all open."

"Perfect," says Frank Einstein.

"So now what?"

Klank staggers through the junkyard door carrying a small mountain of electronics.

He bounces his way off walls and shelves over to the workbench and drops an avalanche of toys, toasters, computers, watches, clocks, radios, clock radios, e-readers, stereo parts, model trains, model planes, model cars, model boats, cameras, waffle makers, humidifiers, scales, talking dolls, telephones, blenders,

heating pads, juicers, sewing machines, drum machines, PlayStations, electric shavers, electric chess sets, electric toothbrushes, hair dryers, range finders, bug zappers, calculators, scanners, DVD players, microwaves, walkie-talkies, and one crawling baby doll.

"Wow," says Frank.

Klink digs himself out from under all the junk Klank has dumped. "What were you thinking?!"

"Thinking?" asks Klank. **"I am doing, not thinking."**

"So what is the invention? Cyber-ware implants? System boosters?" Watson asks.

Frank Einstein looks over the pile of electronics and remotes and human-body notes. He thinks. He nods. He smiles. "Close, Watson. Very close."

Frank Einstein spreads out his invention blueprint and starts to explain his idea . . .

13

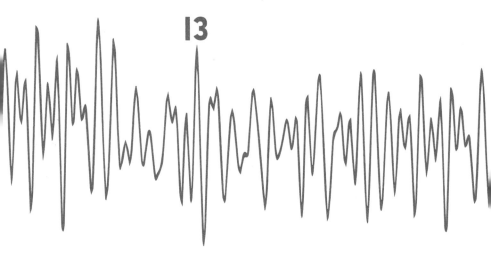

HERE IT IS. MY. BIG. INVENTION!" SAYS T. EDISON. HE POSES proudly in the middle of T. Edison Laboratories Test Room No. 7.

Mr. Chimp looks up from his chess game. Mr. Chimp shakes his head.

Edison doesn't notice. He tightens the strap of the big invention balanced on his head.

"I call it—the T. Edison Brain Swirler."

Mr. Chimp stares. The only thing he can think of is what the Swirler reminds him of—a big toilet.

Igor, the laboratory cat, is not impressed, either. He licks one paw and stretches.

Edison sets up a row of rewired toy ponies, puppies, and hamsters on the test-room lab table.

"It works like a super–remote control and sends signals directly from the brain."

Mr. Chimp takes a black knight with his white bishop. There is so much he would like to say. But all he can do is sign:

B A D

"What?! You don't know what you're talking about. Watch this."

Edison twists on the main power switch (that looks an awful lot like a toilet flush handle).

Edison squints one eye and concentrates on his brain waves.

The plastic pony nods.

Edison turns his brain waves on the puppy.

The puppy barks!

Edison aims the Brain Swirler at the hamster.

It hops!

Edison switches off the Brain Swirler. "Ha! See? I told you!"

Mr. Chimp is not really impressed by a giant remote control for stupid toys that makes you look like you are wearing a toilet on your head.

Mr. Chimp slides his white rook the whole length of the board to check the black king.

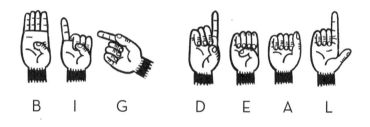

B I G   D E A L

"You are so right it's a big deal," says Edison. "Because I can also use the Edison Brain Swirler to control"—Edison looks around to make sure he is not being overheard—"*brain waves from other brains.*"

Mr. Chimp sits up.

Control brain waves from other brains?

This actually could be a Big Deal.

Mr. Chimp picks up the hopping hamster and signs:

T E S T E D ?

"Well, I haven't had a chance to test it on a real brain yet." Edison gives Mr. Chimp a funny look. "But I think the first live test subject should be . . . you!"

Mr. Chimp is a chimpanzee. But he is not stupid. He signs:

I G O R

"Excellent idea!" Edison picks up Igor and puts the cat on the lab table. Igor licks one paw. "I will start with something simple." Edison flips the Swirler handle to ON. "I will brain-wave command Igor to stand up and meow."

Mr. Chimp gives Edison a thumbs-up . . . and imagines all he might be able to do with brain waves.

Edison adjusts one of the Swirler dials, squints, and thinks, STAND UP.

Igor stands up.

Edison thinks, MEOW.

Igor lifts his head and meows.

Both Edison and Mr. Chimp lean forward.

Edison thinks, TWITCH TAIL.

Igor slowly twitches his tail . . . and then suddenly jumps and spins and jumps and spins and jumps and spins in crazy circles.

Edison cuts off the Swirler.

But Igor keeps jumping and spinning. He jump-spins right off the lab table, out of the test room, and headfirst into a T. Edison Laboratories metal trash can.

Bonnnnng!

Edison staggers backward. The weight of the Brain Swirler tips him back, back, and then completely upside down in one big Brain Swirler smash.

Mr. Chimp's dreams of superpowering his brain waves disappear in the shattered pieces of the Brain Swirler. He drops the motionless hamster and backhands the black king off the chessboard with one short, disappointed, angry *"Oooo!"*

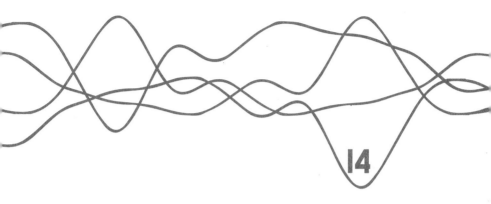

14

HERE IT IS. OUR NEXT INVENTION," SAYS FRANK EINSTEIN IN HIS garage lab.

"Very cool," says Watson.

Frank holds a seriously refitted Midville Mud Hens hat and runs through his invention blueprint one more time.

"**OBSERVATION:** All human-body systems report to the *brain*. All five senses report to the *brain*."

Klink instantly checks the research and confirms. "True."

"The *brain* controls everything."

"True."

"**HYPOTHESIS:** So we might be able to boost human-body perfor-mance by boosting the *brain*."

"Possibly."

Frank continues.

"**EXPERIMENT:** We use the design from the electronics collected by Klank—"

"**Oh yeah! Oh yeah!**" boops Klank, with no re-search but plenty of enthusiasm.

"—the systems of the remotes collected by Watson—"

"Exactly," agrees Watson.

"—and the trick of the turbocharger from Grampa Al's engine work—"

"**Va-voom!**" cheers Klank.

"—to turbocharge brain waves so the brain can boost whatever part of the body you choose!"

"And Janegoodall can boost her muscular system," says Watson.

"Exactly," says Frank. "And there could be a million other ways to use this. Like controlling the FrankenDrone with only brain waves. Making music with no instruments. Moving bi-  onic arms and legs. Helping people like Grampa Al boost their memories."

"And boost people's taste buds?" asks Watson. "So they can taste more candy?"

"Absolutely," answers Frank.

"And boost Janegoodall's muscle strength," says Klink. "So she can pitch faster."

"Exactly," says Frank.

"And boost chickens?" asks Klank. **"So they can cross the road?"**

Frank thinks about this for a second. "No. That's just weird."

Frank Einstein pulls the new Mud Hens cap firmly on his head.

"Robots and Watson, I give you—the BrainTurbo!"

"Ooooh! Ooooh! Let me test it! Let me test it!" says Klank. "I want to turbocharge my brain and be human!"

Frank laughs. "Sorry, Klank, but the BrainTurbo is built to work on human brains. No telling what it might do to an electronic brain."

Watson thumps Klank's metal body. "And you are not exactly human."

"Awww. That makes my circuits sad."

"That is not possible," says Klink.

"We can only test this on a human brain," says Frank, glancing around the lab and ending up looking directly at Watson. "So . . ."

This makes Watson very nervous. Because he and Frank have tested a lot of inventions. And Watson has lost a lot of shoes and clothes, and some hair and skin and pride, in these tests.

"Wow," says Watson. "I really wish I could help, but I . . . uhhh . . . have a headache and I've got a cough and—"

"Only I can test this," says Frank.

"—and these are brand-new pants and . . . What?" says Watson. "I mean, absolutely! You want to test it on yourself, not on me? Great idea!"

Frank walks over to the big mirror on the wall. "Let's start with something simple. Klink and Klank, you observe and measure. Watson, you record."

"Ready," says Klink.

"Set," says Klank.

"Go," says Watson.

Frank clicks the BrainTurbo on. "I will try this move"— he touches his right index finger to his nose—"and see if

I can turbo-boost my muscular system to make it faster. Begin experiment!"

Frank touches his nose.

He dials the Turbo up to 2, then touches his nose again.

"Same speed," reports Klink. "No change."

Watson goes to write the results, but his right hand flies up and smacks his nose. "Hey!"

"Increasing Turbo," says Frank. He twists the dial to 4 and makes the move to his nose again.

Watson's right hand smacks his face twice as fast, twice as hard. "Owwww!"

"Same speed," reports Klink.

"No change," confirms Klank.

"Increasing Turbo to MAX!" says Frank.

"Nooooooo, wait!" says Watson.

Frank sets the dial to 10 and touches his nose three times as fast as he can.

Whack! Whack! Whack! Watson smacks himself three times so fast and so hard that he knocks himself right off his stool.

"Same speed," reports Klink.

"No change," confirms Klank.

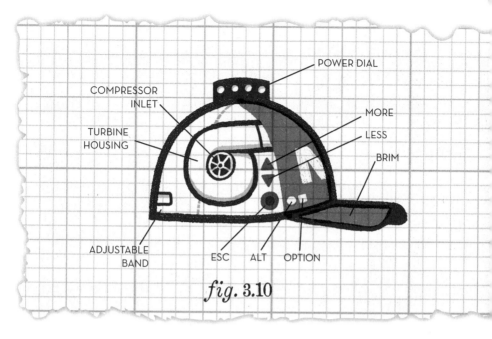

fig. **3.10**

Frank takes off the BrainTurbo and brings it to the workbench. He checks the connections and circuits. "Take this down, Watson. **ANALYSIS:** Something appears to be wrong with the wiring. Boosted brain signals not getting to muscular system."

"Oooooooooh," says Watson from the floor.

"What are you doing down there, Watson? Stop goofing around and help us with the experiment."

Watson crawls back up on his stool, a little dizzy from the beating his own right hand has given him. "The boosted brain signals were working fine. They were just working in the wrong direction—on *me* instead of on *you*."

Frank rechecks the BrainTurbo's wiring. "Aha! Brilliant, Watson. And just like Grampa Al always says—failure is success in progress."

"Great," says Watson, wiping his bruised nose.

Frank flips the connections on the BrainTurbo to redirect the boosted brain signals. He pulls on the hat, sets the Turbo dial to 5, and touches his nose in an almost invisible blur.

"Five times faster than base speed!" reports Klink.

"Success!" confirms Klank.

"OK, that really is genius," marvels Watson, rubbing his smacked nose.

"Now for the real test," says Frank. "Call Janegoodall. Have her meet us at the ballpark in five minutes."

15

TEDISON STANDS LOOKING OUT THE GLASS WALL OF THE T. EDISON Laboratories tower. He watches the Midville citizens, small as ants below.

"Such a waste of brainpower. People just don't know how to use their brains."

Mr. Chimp picks through the broken pieces of the Edison Brain Swirler. He compares the wiring to a chart of human brain waves he has printed out.

He sees where the Swirler went wrong.

He daydreams again his biggest Mr. Chimp dreams.

"Dunderheads," mutters Edison. "They would be so much better off if I controlled what they thought."

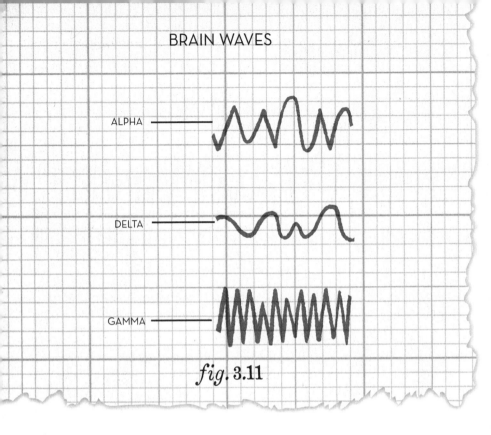

BRAIN WAVES

ALPHA

DELTA

GAMMA

fig. 3.11

"*Meoorrrrrrwwww,*" says Igor, curled up on Edison's office chair, his head freshly bandaged.

"If only I could control their brain waves. But how?"

Mr. Chimp gives a shrug. There is no way he wants to help fix any part of a toilet-shaped invention called a Swirler. Mr. Chimp has brain waves, and ideas, and plans of his own.

Edison slaps his hand on the window in frustration. He kicks the base of the super-binoculars, then occupies him-

self by spotting everyone all over Midville wasting their brainpower again.

"Woman sniffing flowers—ninnyhammer! Man staring at painting—dimwit!"

Mr. Chimp quietly connects a net of wires, circuits, and sensors inside a fancy black top hat. He flips a small switch, spots the headless baby doll in the pile of toy wreckage, and thinks, CRAWL.

"Chowderhead nincompoops in the baseball park," gripes Edison from the binocular perch. "Wait a minute. Those nincompoops are Einstein and his numskull dumbots."

The headless baby shuffles on its hands and knees . . . and crawls out of the pile.

"And that girl throwing the baseball . . . They better be working on getting me my money."

Mr. Chimp adjusts his top hat at a jaunty angle and thinks, DANCE.

"Why are they all jumping around? Holding up her baseball cap . . . Hmmm . . . Well, look at that . . . That is no ordinary baseball cap . . . Very interesting . . ."

The headless baby dances.

"Mr. Chimp!" calls a very excited T. Edison. "I think I

have found the answer to our brain-control question! And a way for Einstein to pay me back!"

"*Ooook*," says Mr. Chimp, in a completely uninterested way, brushing his fancy black top hat.

"This means a mission for you tonight."

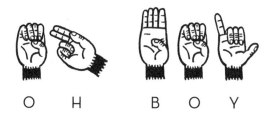

O H   B O Y

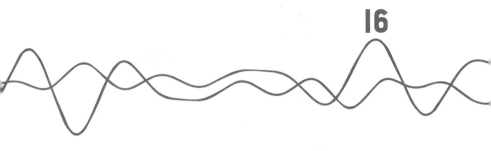

16

NIGHT.

The Midville Mud Hens tryouts are tomorrow at noon. So Janegoodall lies at home in her bed, in the first stage of sleep, happily thinking of her sixty-mile-per-hour fastball, pulsing alpha brain waves as she begins to drift off.

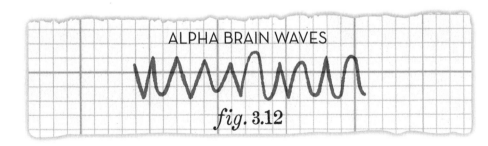

ALPHA BRAIN WAVES

fig. 3.12

Watson lies at home in his bed, dropping into the second and third stages of sleep, heartbeat slowing, temperature dropping, thinking of inventing a candy that has every taste, then thinking absolutely nothing, delta brain waving.

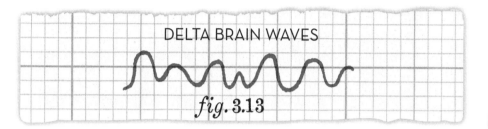

DELTA BRAIN WAVES

fig. 3.13

Frank Einstein lies upstairs in his bed at Grampa Al's, in deep rapid-eye-movement sleep, voluntary muscles all but paralyzed, brain consuming more oxygen now than when completely awake, making connections and solving problems in shifting, throbbing colors and images, patterns and sounds, in gamma-brain-wave dreaming.

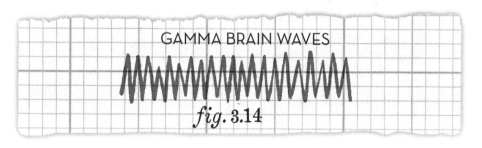

GAMMA BRAIN WAVES

fig. 3.14

Klink sits in the corner of the lab, shut down, plugged into his favorite outlet, filling up on his favorite 120-volt AC power.

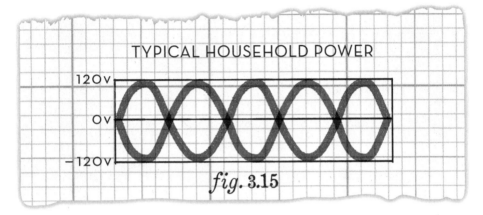

TYPICAL HOUSEHOLD POWER

fig. 3.15

Klank, however, is *not* in his favorite La-Z-Boy recharger recliner.

Klank is pacing back and forth in front of the lab door, guarding the BrainTurbo on the lab workbench.

Klank whispers to himself, **"Frank Einstein says, 'Guard the BrainTurbo.' I must guard the BrainTurbo."**

Klank walks back and forth, back and forth, back and forth. He is an alert guard. He is a good guard. The BrainTurbo is an amazing invention.

Klank paces.

Klank thinks he should take a closer look at the BrainTurbo. He paces over to the workbench and stares down at it. A hat that turbocharges brain power. Amazing.

It might be safer if he held it. Klank picks up the BrainTurbo.

"Mmmmm," rumbles Klank.

Klank feels a spark of an idea. Or at least a spark of part of an idea.

OK—he's got one word.

Klank whispers the word to himself, like a wish:

"Human."

Klank swivels his head around in a complete 360 to make sure no one is watching. He carefully places the BrainTurbo on his vegetable-strainer head.

A good guard would make sure the BrainTurbo was still working.

Klank turns on the BrainTurbo with a faint *tick*.

In the corner, Klink gives a quick electro-beep snort.

A good guard would not disturb Klink's recharge. A good guard would take the BrainTurbo outside.

Klank turns and sneaks—as quietly as a large metal robot can sneak—out the front laboratory door. He eases the door softly click-shut behind him.

Klank leans against the brick storefront of Grampa Al's Fix It! shop and turns the BrainTurbo dial to 1.

Electrical impulses surge, and double, and surge again into Klank's vegetable-strainer head.

"Oooooooooooh," hums Klank.

Klank is flooded with turbocharged inputs: the golden lights of downtown Midville in the distance, beautiful sounds, a riot of thrilling flower-earth-life smells in the spring night air.

Almost overcome by these turbocharged new robot senses, Klank staggers toward the night sights and sounds and smells . . . and never notices the shadowy barefoot figure in the fancy black top hat following him.

17

HUMANS. DEEP IN THE OLDEST JUNGLE. DENSE GREEN. BIRDCALLS *echo. Wet earth smell. Mud squishes through toes. Air thick enough to taste. Following a skeleton hiker. That suddenly lights up a network of sparking nerves, feeding into a glowing brain. A clearing ahead. There—a dark fig-ure, from the future, stands on a mound of sand, winds up, and fires a rock . . . fast, faster, fastest . . .* dreams Janegoodall.

Candy. Sweet, sour, salty, bitter, hot, cold, glorious. Turbocharged candy. Pulsing, exploding super candy . . . dreams Watson.

The watery crash of ocean waves. Schools of . . . those fish . . . not really fish . . . what do you call those things? Bottlenose mammals leap out of the water in graceful arcs. The blue-green water covering Earth. The solar system of Mercury, Venus, Mars . . . and that next planet. Used to know them like my own name . . . dreams Grampa Al.

Purple storm clouds crashing over volcano lightning-bolt drumming heartbeat explosion. Grab that blue-white crackling electrical charge. Guide it into looping spiral. Multiply it through brain stem, to brain lobes in a beautiful, throbbing, golden network. Janegoodall cheers. Watson laughs. Grampa Al, but somehow ten-year-old Grampa Al, dances a funny little dance . . . dreams Frank Einstein.

01010111 01001000 01011001 00100000
01000011 01001000 01001001 01000011
01001011 01000101 01001110 00100000
01010111 01001000 01011001 00111111 . . .
dreams Klink.

18

NEON LIGHTS! RED AND GREEN AND YELLOW AND PURPLE!

Music! Rock and salsa and jazz and blues!

Humans strolling in the warm, jasmine-scented spring night air. The smell of popcorn sharp enough to taste.

Klank hops a quick dance step.

Klank opens his arms and sings, **"I am going to wang dang doodle. All night long."**

Klank tugs the BrainTurbo tight on his head. A good guard would make sure the BrainTurbo worked at higher power. He twists the dial up to 3.

Klank feels the increased charge from his head to the rest of his body. The colors and sounds and smells of downtown

Midville are suddenly, intensely, beautifully sharp and true and right.

Klank feels an urge to share this beauty. He sees a man and woman dancing in a gorgeous hotel lobby. They are so perfectly electric. Klank will go with them!

Or that group of boys, wrestling and joking. Klank knows jokes! The boys climb into a bus and roar off into the night.

Klank hugs a mailbox, leaving it in a whole new shape.

Klank hop-skips down the street, humming to himself, taking in sparkling stars, majestic trees, soaring buildings, and then . . . Oh.

He sees her.

She is in the window of Ace's Hardware.

Her face glows with a knowing smile. Her blue eyes sparkle. Her shape, her curves, her dials and switches. Her arms exactly like Klank's arm!

She holds out a flower.

Klank is pretty sure she says, "Do you want to play with me?"

"Uhhhhhhhh," says Klank, suddenly unable to speak a real sentence.

But Klank does want to play with her, so he pushes a panel of the window. It swings open. She smiles.

"Ahhhhhh," says Klank, still completely tongue-tied.

A gust of wind blows the flower out of her hand. Klank beeps. **"Mmmmmm?"**

The intoxicating warm spring wind gusts again.

Her head nods.

Klank steps into the front window and takes her hand. He pulls her to him . . . and pops her hand completely off.

Klank stops, stumbles. He tries to put her hand back on her arm.

The arm drops with a crash and a clatter.

Humans down the street are looking Klank's way.

Klank puts his arm around her. Her leg falls off! Klank scoops up legs and arms and head and torso. He hears a man yelling now. Klank turns, off balance, and stumbles out the window and into the street.

Arms, legs, and torso fall, leaving Klank holding nothing but her head.

The streetlight flickers.

"EEEEEEeeeeeeeeeee!" a woman screams. "That poor woman! It's a monster!"

Klank looks up. **"NO!"** he says, or tries to say.

But what comes out is **"RRRRRROOOOOOOAAAARRRRR!"**

"A monster!"

Now it's three humans, four, ten, more.

Klank panics.

He drops her head with a hollow *thunk*.

"Monster!"

Klank thinks he should stay and explain. Klank thinks he should run away. Klank doesn't know what to think.

A dark top-hatted figure drops from the shadows above. The figure takes Klank's hand, gives a soft "*ooook*," and pulls Klank toward the alley.

"Monster!"

Klank, his BrainTurbo throbbing, gladly follows.

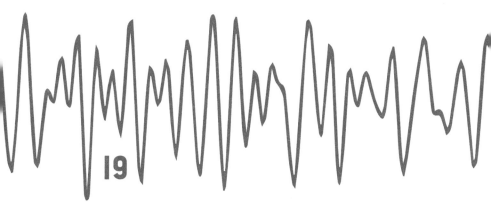

19

BY THE TIME FRANK GETS DOWN TO THE KITCHEN FOR BREAKFAST, Watson is already on his third helping of Grampa Al's classic French toast.

"Good morning, Einstein," says Grampa Al, whisking a splash of milk into a bowl of beaten eggs.

"Good morning, Einstein," answers a still-sleepy Frank.

"Good morning, Watson," says Watson.

Frank plops down in a kitchen chair and shakes his head. "That doesn't make sense, Watson."

Frank rubs his eyes, then his whole skull. "Why is it so hard to get started in the morning?"

Grampa Al dips three pieces of his homemade bread into the egg-and-milk mixture. "Takes a lot to get our brains and bodies going again after we shut down for sleep. Like starting a cold car engine. Got to give it some fuel to burn to get going."

Grampa Al drops the soaked bread slices into the butter sizzling in the frying pan.

"It's kind of weird that we conk out and do nothing for eight hours every day," Frank thinks out loud. "We could get a lot more done if we kept going twenty-four hours a day."

"Hey, yeah," says Watson. "Why *do* we sleep?"

"That is a great question," says Grampa Al. "Scientists know that every animal sleeps in some way. And if you don't sleep, your body breaks down, and your brain goes haywire." Grampa Al flips over the bread slices. "But nobody really knows why we sleep. Or why we dream."

"That's crazy," says Watson.

Grampa Al picks up the pan, forks a golden, buttery piece of French toast, and drops it onto Watson's plate.

"And that's beautiful," says Watson. "More fuel for my engine!"

"But don't scientists who study sleep have some ideas?" asks Frank.

"Do dogs have fleas?" answers Grampa Al, forking Frank his piece of toast. "One idea is called Restore and Repair. That the brain and body use sleep time to fix themselves."

Grampa Al looks around the kitchen. "Now where did I put my fork . . . ?"

"It's in your hand."

"Yikes! Right," Grampa Al forks the last piece of French toast onto his own plate. "Second idea is that the brain and body slow down in this sleep state to conserve energy."

"Mmmmmm."

Frank, Watson, and Grampa Al trance out, using touch, taste, sight, and smell senses to completely enjoy their French toast drizzled with Grampa Al's very own maple syrup.

"And third," Grampa Al says, picking up where he left

off, "the brain uses dream time to process information it learned during the day and locks it into long-term memory."

Watson thinks about this. "So do robots dream?"

"Absolutely," answers Grampa Al.

"Of electric sheep?" adds Frank.

Frank and Grampa Al laugh.

"Which reminds my sputtering brain—Watson tells me you guys perfected both your BrainTurbo and his da Vinci!"

Frank gulps the last of his sweet and buttery breakfast. His digestive system starts working to break down the food and fuel his body and brain. "Just in time. Mud Hens tryouts are this afternoon. We took the idea of your turbocharger and used it on the brain."

"Well, paint me red and call me Shirley!"

"Huh?" says Watson.

"Come on, Watson," calls Frank, already halfway out the kitchen door, heading for the lab. "I told Janegoodall we'd meet her at the ballpark early. So we better make like trees . . . and leave."

"Ohhhhh no," says Watson.

"Or make like lightning . . . and bolt," adds Grampa Al.

"Or make like dogs and flea."

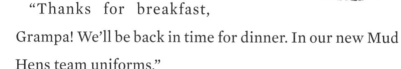

"Or make like DNA and split."

"Thanks for breakfast, Grampa! We'll be back in time for dinner. In our new Mud Hens team uniforms."

Frank and Watson run to the lab, ready to go. And ready to show the world what the BrainTurbo can do.

They fall into the lab. "Rise and shine, Klink and Klank! Time to make like bananas and split!" calls Frank.

"Time to make like tires . . . and hit the road," adds Watson, getting the hang of it.

"RRRRRhuh?" Klink, plugged into the outlet in the corner, powers up.

"Klink! Where is Klank? He was supposed to be guarding the BrainTurbo," says Frank.

Klink quickly scans the entire lab and sonar-sweeps all of Grampa Al's for any sign of Klank. "Klank is not here."

Watson stares at the empty workbench. "And where is the BrainTurbo?"

Klink rescans . . . resweeps. And then bluntly confirms Frank and Watson's worst fear.

"The BrainTurbo is not here."

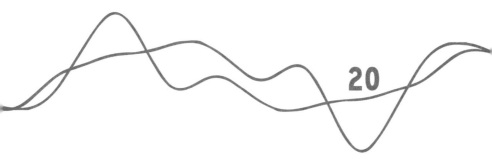

20

FRANK FLIES HIS ANTIMATTER MOTOR FLY BIKE OVER ALL OF NORTH Midville.

Klank is not there. The BrainTurbo is not there.

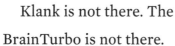

Watson searches South Midville on the maglev skateboard.

No Klank or BrainTurbo there.

Janegoodall covers East Midville.

No and nothing.

Grampa Al and Klink turbo-truck search West Midville.

Zilch and nada.

Time is up.

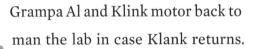

Grampa Al and Klink motor back to man the lab in case Klank returns. And to look for clues they might have missed.

Frank, Watson, and Janegoodall meet outside the ballpark. Time for the tryouts.

"It's all my fault," says Watson. "I never should have told Klank he wasn't human. Do you think that's what made him take off?"

Frank slaps a baseball into his glove. "It's not your fault, Watson. You were just telling him the truth. He isn't human."

"Sorry we let you down, J."

"No worries," says Janegoodall. "We'll find that big lunk after the tryouts."

Frank checks his watch. "Klank may not be the smartest robot. But he is a robot, absolutely loyal to his mission. I'm sure he's somewhere following his orders."

"But where?" asks Watson. "And where is the BrainTurbo?"

Frank looks at the huge sign behind them. "The one place we haven't looked?"

"Klank hates Edison and his ape. He would be out of his robot mind to go there!" says Watson.

"Hmmmm," says Frank, pulling on his baseball cap. "Exactly . . ."

"MIDVILLE MUD HENS!" booms the public-address speakers inside Midville Menlo Park. "Let the tryouts begin!"

21

WHAT USED TO BE THE BRAINTURBO SITS DELICATELY ATOP an electronic head.

The electronic head fits securely bolted to a large robot body.

The large robot body lies firmly strapped to a tilted operating table.

A tiny wisp of smoke curls into the air above the robot's head and vanishes.

"There," says T. Edison, powering down a wired baseball cap and taking it off the robot's head. "That didn't hurt a bit now, did it, Klank?"

Klank runs a quick electrical charge through his head circuits, his heart circuits, and his body circuits. Something is different.

"Owwww," says Klank. **"That . . . hurt."**

"Well, of course it's going to hurt *a little bit*," says T. Edison impatiently. "You don't get to be what you want to be without *some* pain."

Mr. Chimp nods and signs:

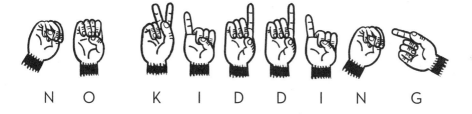

N O   K I D D I N G

Klank blinks. He is not so sure. **"More human?"**

T. Edison checks the charts and graphs from the operation. "A little adjustment, a few improvements in that shoddy Einstein TurkeyBrain hat—and now we have a *real* invention!"

Edison holds up the rewired BrainTurbo. "It will improve the weak-brained . . . and guide the wrong-brained . . . just the way I want them to behave. I call it—the Edison BrainWaver! What do you think?"

Mr. Chimp thinks the Edison BrainWaver looks exactly like Einstein's BrainTurbo, but with a big *E* instead of an *M* written on the hat.

Klank hums and thinks for a second.

Klank answers, **"To be, or not to be, that is the question . . ."**

Mr. Chimp nods.

"Whether 'tis nobler in the mind to suffer the slings and arrows of outrageous fortune . . ."

Edison unbuckles the thick leather straps restraining Klank.

". . . Or to take arms against a sea of troubles . . ."

Mr. Chimp helps Klank down.

". . . And by opposing, end them."

Klank looks out the window, down at the tiny humans in the Midville ballpark below.

"To die: to sleep—"

Klank goes quiet.

"Very impressive," says T. Edison.

Klank doesn't know exactly where this has come from.

But it makes his circuits buzz with a hard-to-pinpoint unease. **"Go, Dog. Go!?"**

"Not exactly," says T. Edison. "Shakespeare."

Edison and Klank watch the humans in the baseball park for a minute. Edison awkwardly puts his arm around Klank's midsection.

"Well, my new thinking-and-feeling robot friend, what do you say we take our new, improved brains out for a little stroll?"

Mr. Chimp shoots Edison a seriously unhappy look. But Edison is too thrilled with himself and his new invention to notice.

"What do you say we go down there and show who's *not* a monster? Show who *is* a genius. And show these humans how to win brains and influence people!"

Edison pats Klank on the back with a metallic *bonk!*

"I am not a monster," says Klank.

"*Ooooh ooook*," huffs Mr. Chimp.

"Oh—and you can come too, Mr. Chimp."

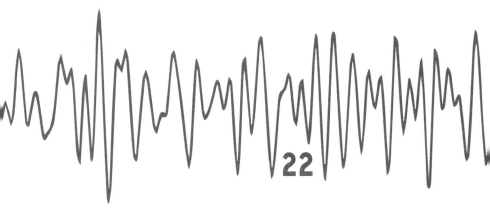

22

O K, PEOPLE," CALLS POLICE CHIEF AND HEAD COACH JACOBS FROM the bench. "Let's see if you got what it takes to be a Midville Mud Hen. Batter up!"

Janegoodall turns sideways to home plate. She folds her arms close to her chest, lifting her left leg in a windup.

"Bring the heat, JG!" calls Watson from his position at second base.

Janegoodall strides forward. She pushes off the mound with her right leg, unfolding her arms, turning her body, extending and windmilling her right arm, and releasing the baseball from her right hand.

"Smoke it!" yells Frank Einstein from his position in center field.

The ball flies from the tips of Janegoodall's fingers and across the forty-six feet to home plate in just over half a second.

Little Harry Abrams closes his eyes, swings the bat completely blind, and makes lucky contact with the ball about to zip past him at fifty-five miles per hour.

Craaaaack!

The baseball rebounds off the bat and rockets up over Janegoodall's head, past second base and into center field, heading for the wall. Frank turns his back to home plate and runs as fast as he can. He stretches out his glove, dives, and . . . *pock!* The ball drops right into a tough, leathery hand . . . with no glove on it.

Frank picks himself up off the outfield grass. "Mr. Chimp? T. Edison? Klank! I knew it!"

Watson and Janegoodall run out to center field.

"Klank! You're safe!" yells Watson, jumping on Klank and giving him a big hug.

"We looked everywhere for you," says Janegoodall. "Are you OK?"

Klank peels Watson off and drops him like a used rag. **"Why would I not be OK? I am, in fact, much better, and now much smarter, than OK. No thanks to you three."**

"Klank?" says Frank Einstein, questioning.

"Klank!" says Janegoodall, scolding.

"Klaaaaank," says Watson, begging.

"That is my name," says Klank, in a completely un-funny way. **"Do not wear it out."**

Watson turns to the kid with the goofy-looking haircut sticking out from under his baseball hat. "Edison, you rat! What did you do to Klank?"

The rest of the tryout players gather around to see what is going on with the chimp and the robot in center field.

Little Maria Karloff points at Klank, takes a deep breath, and screams, "*EEEeeeeeeeeeee!* That's the monster! The one I saw ripping the doll lady to pieces. *EEEEeeeeeee!*"

Klank steps back in fear.

Edison grits his teeth and squints his eyes at the piercing sound of Maria's scream.

"*EEEEEEeeeeeeeeee!* A monster!"

"Oh, for goodness' sake," says Edison, "*shut up!*"

Maria is shocked quiet. "We don't say shut up."

"Well, good for you," says Edison. "Because *I do! And I just did! So zip it!* This is not a monster. This is my robot, Klank. He *used* to be a monster. When he had a bad brain given to him by this kid—Frank Einstein. But I helped Klank. And now he is smart and a fine citizen. All because of my new invention."

Edison pulls a cap covered in electrodes and wires out of his back pocket. He holds it up for all the baseball players to see.

"I call it the Edison BrainWaver!"

"What?!" yells Watson. "No way! That's Frank Einstein's BrainTurbo! And you stole it!"

"Did not."

"Did too!"

"Did not."

"You *did*!"

"But it has my *E* right here—
E for Edison. See?"

"*Ooook!*" adds Mr. Chimp.

"Great balls of fire!" yells Chief
Coach Jacobs, pushing through the
crowd of kids. "What is this, some
kind of sewing circle? Or is this
baseball tryouts?!"

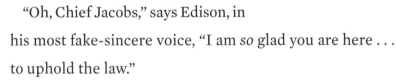

"Oh, Chief Jacobs," says Edison, in
his most fake-sincere voice, "I am *so* glad you are here . . .
to uphold the law."

"Yeah," says Watson. "Edison is a crook. He stole Frank
Einstein's invention. And his robot. Arrest him!"

"I just want what's best for the Midville Mud Hens. And
with my Edison BrainWaver, I promise you that this fine
citizen"—Edison puts his arm around Klank—"can make
us a winning team."

"A robot?" says Chief Coach Jacobs. "Playing baseball?"

"There is nothing in the *InterCity Baseball Rule Book* **that would bar me from participating,"** says Klank.

Chief Coach Jacobs whips out his copy of the rule book and reads aloud. "Hmmm . . . 'Players must be eleven years old or younger as of today's date, and a resident of the town of Midville proper.'"

"I am younger than eleven years," beeps Klank. **"And I am a resident of Midville proper."**

"And with the Edison BrainWaver," adds Edison, "he is better than humans at everything! A most amazing batter and catcher and . . . pitcher."

"Also most intelligent," brags Klank. **"I have passed the Turing test, which determines whether an intelligence is robot or human. And just this morning I beat Watson, IBM's supercomputer, in chess. Five hundred and twenty-seven times."**

Watson turns to Frank. "Did he really just say 'most intelligent'? And is IBM's supercomputer really named Watson?"

Frank shakes his head. "Something happened to Klank in Edison's laboratory."

Chief Coach Jacobs takes his hat off and scratches his head. "Well, I'll be a monkey's uncle."

Mr. Chimp rocks restlessly from foot to foot.

"It is not a good sign when chimps do that," Janegoodall whispers to Chief Coach Jacobs. "It might be best to let them do what they want."

"OK! Enough of this chewing the fat!" Jacobs sputters. "We've got tryouts! Let's see some pitching! Everybody—move it!"

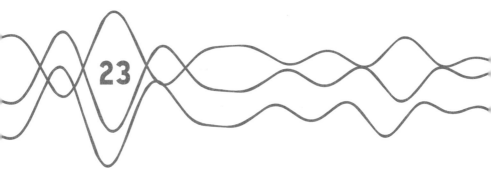

23

KLANK TURNS SIDEWAYS TO HOME PLATE. HE FOLDS HIS ARMS close to his chest, lifting his left leg in a windup.

Frank, and Watson, and Janegoodall watch from the home dugout.

"This is very weird," says Watson, unwrapping a hot dog and chomping on it.

Klank strides forward. He pushes off the mound with his right leg, unfolding his arms, turning his body, extending and windmilling his right arm, and releasing the baseball from his right hand.

"Edison is up to something," says Frank Einstein. "He is not doing this just to help Klank join the Mud Hens."

The ball flies from the tips of Klank's fingers in a blur.

Poooom! The ball pops into the catcher's mitt with a puff of dirt.

"Wonderful pitch," says T. Edison from the visitors' dugout.

Chief Coach Jacobs checks the radar gun. "Sixty. Not too shabby."

"This is just wrong," says Janegoodall, gripping her baseball in a four-seam fastball hold. "He is a machine."

T. Edison hops out of the dugout. He talks to Chief Coach Jacobs, who shrugs. "Knock yourself out."

Edison walks out to the mound, carrying the Edison BrainWaver.

"What is he doing . . . ?" asks Frank.

From the pitcher's mound, Edison announces to everyone at the Mud Hens tryouts, "You may have thought that was good. But I want to show you that the Edison BrainWaver can be *great.*" He hands the boosted baseball cap to Klank.

"Oh, this is not good," says Frank.

Klank puts on the Edison BrainWaver and dials it up to 3.

"So not good."

Klank winds up again and fires a pitch.

Pooom!

"Seventy miles per hour!" calls Chief Coach Jacobs.

Klank dials to 4 and pitches again.

Pooom!

"Eighty!"

Klank dials to 5 and pitches again.

Pooom!

"Ninety! We have us a fastballer! Throwing some cheese!"

"Grrrrrrrrrr," says Janegoodall.

Watson's eyes almost bug out of his head. "I thought you said the turbocharger didn't work on robot brains."

Frank calculates. "It can . . . up to a point. But too much boosting sets up an irreversible feedback loop that overloads pathways and results in catastrophic disintegrative combustion."

Watson gulps the last of his hot dog and drops the foil wrapper on the dugout floor. "It feeds the reverse of what?"

"It will explode Klank's head. To smithereens."

Watson wipes the mustard off his lips and glares at Edison. "No! That is terrible. Hey! Now what are they up to?"

Edison takes the cap from Klank. "Now I am going to show you something even more astounding about the Edison BrainWaver." Edison points Klank off the mound and back to the dugout. Then he dramatically places the BrainWaver on his own head—and without letting anyone see, clicks the WAVE ARROW DIRECTION from IN to OUT.

"The Edison BrainWaver doesn't just enhance brains . . . it also *connects* them! Allow me to demonstrate."

"Aha," says Frank. "So that's it."

Frank picks up Watson's hot dog wrapper from the dugout floor.

"What's *it*?" asks Watson.

But before Frank can explain, T. Edison turns and yells from the mound, "Watson! Will you please come out and help me?"

"No way," says Watson's mouth. But Watson's body jumps up and strolls out to the mound.

Edison dials the BrainWaver up to 6. "Watch what happens when I think, SKIP, WATSON."

Watson skips.

"Or—DANCE, WATSON."

Watson steps a little dance.

Edison dials the BrainWaver to 7. He beams his brain waves off the cell phone towers on the ballpark roof, boosting and broadcasting his thoughts wide enough to cover everyone in the ballpark.

Edison thinks, *This is good. Edison is good. All is good.*

Watson, Chief Coach Jacobs, and Janegoodall think, *All is good.*

Connor, Mike, Ashley, and Joey think, *All is good.*

Jennifer, Wally, Mac, Daniel, Oliver, Mo, Jackie, Steve, and every single person in the stadium thinks, *All . . . is . . . good.*

"Everyone nod!" Edison thinks and says.

Everyone nods.

"Everyone wave!" Edison thinks and says.

Everyone waves.

"Success!" Edison laughs. "Brain control!" Edison laughs harder. "Watson—chicken dance!"

Watson tucks his hands in his armpits, flaps his elbows, and hop-steps around in circles in a very awful-looking chicken dance.

Edison laughs.

And laughs.

And laughs.

24

EDISON STANDS ON THE MIDVILLE MUD HENS PITCHING MOUND, nodding his head and waving his arms like some kind of demented brain-wave conductor.

Edison thinks.

His brain waves pulse.

Janegoodall twirls in a circle.

Edison thinks.

His brain waves pulse.

Chief Coach Jacobs picks his nose.

Mr. Chimp sits in the visitors' dugout, legs crossed, finishing his sudoku puzzle.

Klank sits next to Mr. Chimp. **"Why is he still doing this? The demonstration worked. The BrainWaver improves brain and body. The BrainWaver controls other brains."**

Edison raises both arms.

His brain waves pulse.

Everyone chants, "Edison is good! Edison is good! Edison is good!"

Mr. Chimp answers Klank, signing:

Klank searches his circuits for understanding. The closest thing he can find is a pattern in his HugMeMonkey! brain.

"Like needing a hug?"

Mr. Chimp looks up from his puzzle, surprised. He looks out at Edison, circling the infield to the chants of "Edison is good! Edison is good!" Mr. Chimp fills in a 7 and nods.

Edison stops the chant. He struts over to Mr. Chimp and Klank. He puts one foot up on the bench and taps his Edison BrainWaver.

"Well? Who's the genius now? These puddingheads don't even know they are being controlled!"

Mr. Chimp signs:

Edison completely ignores Mr. Chimp. "So, first—I will make them like me. Second—I will make them buy every Edison product on the market. And third—I think I will have everyone elect me . . . mayor! Yes, mayor of Midville."

Mr. Chimp shakes his head. He is thinking, *What a waste of a great invention*. But Mr. Chimp doesn't say or sign anything.

Klank says truthfully, **"Yes, that is all possible."**

"You better believe it's possible, metalhead," says Edison, spitting like the major league player he thinks he is. "But I will need more power, more range. How do I boost this more?"

Edison spits again. He looks across the infield and sees his answer sitting in the home dugout. "Humpty and Dumpty! Come over here!"

Einstein and Watson look blankly back at Edison.

"Nitwits! I mean you two—Einstein and Watson! Come over here!"

Frank Einstein and Watson half stumble, kind of sleep-walk over to the visitors' dugout.

"Frank Einstein. Tsk, tsk, tsk," spits Edison. "It's kind of a shame it had to end this way. It was more fun battling you when you were a genius, too. But now everyone loves genius *me*. And everyone hates monster-builder *you*."

Frank just blinks.

"Oh well. That's the way the genius crumbles."

T. Edison stands nose to nose with Frank Einstein. He looks Frank in the eye. Frank looks back with a dull stare.

Watson bobs his head, still doing a bit of a chicken dance.

"But before I destroy you, tell me, Einstein. Is there any way to increase the range of the BrainTurbo—I mean the Edison BrainWaver? To reach the whole town?"

Frank Einstein nods. "Yes."

Watson clucks.

"The whole country?"

Frank Einstein nods. "Yes."

Watson cluck, clucks.

"The whole world?"

Frank Einstein nods. "Yes."

Watson cluck, cluck, clucks.

"And how might we—I—do that?"

Frank looks over at Klank. "You can increase both power and range by amplifying a robot brain. By turning the setting to MAX."

"*Bawk bawk bawwwwwk!*" says Watson.

"Yes!" says Edison, taking off the BrainWaver. "I mean—that's exactly what I thought!"

Mr. Chimp rolls his eyes.

"But," continues Frank, "it may be dangerous. Your brain waves will overpower all other brain waves."

Edison freezes. "Oh gosh! What a terrible problem! I will be controlling everyone's brains. Let me think carefully if I should do that!"

Edison puts his hand to his chin for exactly one second.

"OK, done. Let's do this. Now."

Frank turns to Klank. "It would be best to have your robot double-check the calculations. For safety."

Watson digs at the dirt with his toes. *"Buk buk buk . . ."*

Edison hands the BrainWaver to Klank. Klank puts the BrainWaver on his head. He runs the calculations. He sees exactly what will happen.

Klank looks at Frank.

Frank looks at Klank. And winks.

Klank is completely confused. This makes no sense. Something is not right. Klank is flooded with signals and pulses from his new, improved head to his old HugMeMonkey! brain and back again.

Klank looks up the meaning of *wink*.

verb

1. to close and open one eye quickly, typically to indicate that something is a joke or a secret, or as a signal of affection.

"All right already, you slow-bot," says T. Edison. "Calculations check. Can you do this? Yes or no?"

Frank looks away.

Watson is now pecking the ground with his nose.

Klank will have to decide this on his own.

Joke? Secret? Signal of affection?

Klank reruns his calculation of what will happen. There is no mistake.

Klank says . . . **"No."**

25

ELECTRIC SHEEP LEAP OVER A WAVEFORM ENERGY FENCE—*ONE,*
two, three . . . millions, billions, trillions.
Ocean waves crash blue warm salty wet.
The sun beams yellow, delicious heat.
Planets revolve around the pulsing sun.
Galaxies of sparkling stars slowly spiral.
She holds out her hand. Klank takes it. The universe inside
him expands to fill the universe outside and beyond.

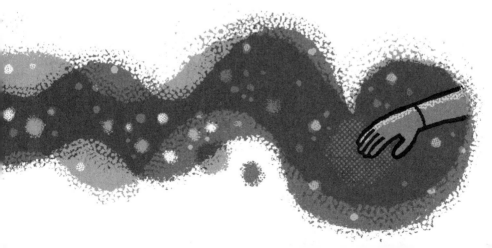

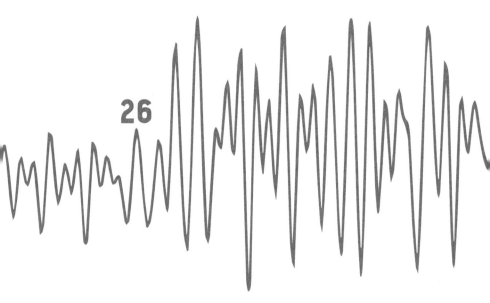

26

EDISON STAMPS HIS FOOT, THEN KICKS DIRT AT KLANK.

"What do you mean, 'no'? I want more range! I want more power! I want control!"

Frank starts to raise one hand, but Klank snaps out of his daydream.

"I mean *no*," says Klank calmly. **"The range and power cannot be increased from this position."**

Frank lowers his hand.

Watson picks up a wriggling worm. And eats it.

"I must position myself in the middle of this recreational field for best results."

Mr. Chimp looks from Klank to Frank and back to Klank.

Mr. Chimp narrows his eyes and opens his nostrils wide, trying to sense what is not quite right.

"Well," says Edison, "what are you waiting for? Christmas? Get out there and crank that thing to MAX!"

Klank nods. Klank follows Edison's orders.

Klank walks slowly out to center field, taking in the smell of grass, the warmth of the sun, the sight of puffy white clouds against such a perfectly blue sky. He sees a tiny red flower and stoops his large robot body to pick it.

"Come *on*!" yells Edison. "Sometime *today* would be nice!"

Klank walks, turns, and plants his feet. He secures the BrainWaver on his head and turns the dial to 8.

The sudden surge of multiplying charges lights and heats Klank's whole metal self.

"Oh yes!" cheers Edison. "More, more, more!"

Klank remembers: *To be, or not to be.*

Klank turns the BrainWaver dial to MAX.

Electrical charges fire from spot to spot, double through the neuro-turbocharger—grow bigger, grow faster, grow stronger . . . hotter . . . more, more, more. And again and again and more and more and too much more.

Klank catches Frank Einstein's eye. Klank winks. And—

Klank's head power-
overloads and explodes
in an instant, all-consuming

BrainWaver/Klank/tiny-red-flower vaporizing flash.

"What?!" cries T. Edison. "Noooooooooooo! My invention is gone!"

"Yuck!" spits Watson. "Who put this
slimy dirt in my mouth?"

"Klank," says Frank. "He really
was more human."

Mr. Chimp nods and signs:

O   R   A   P   E

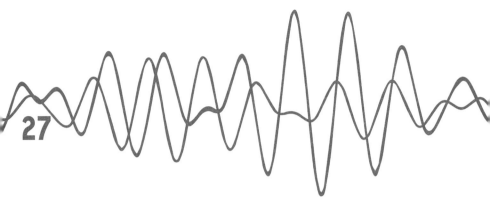

27

MERCURY. VENUS. EARTH. MARS. JUPITER. SATURN. URANUS. Neptune." Grampa Al rattles off the names of the planets. He wiggles the rebuilt Brain-Turbo on his head.

"Wow! This is the bee's knees!"

Janegoodall laughs. "Bees have knees?"

Grampa Al is too excited to answer. "Let me see if I can remember the names of different bones—humerus, radius, ulna, carpals! Ooh, ooh—parts of the brain! Cerebrum, cerebellum, medulla oblongata!"

Grampa Al holds his head, and the BrainTurbo, in both hands. "Hammer, pliers, screwdriver, wrench! Ratchet, saw, punch, file, drill! It's all coming back to me now. This bit of headgear could change *everything*. Just think of kids with learning problems, old fogies like me losing memory, anybody with any brain challenge . . . You have done something really good here, Frank Einstein," says Grampa Al, proudly hugging Frank.

"But I still don't get it," says Watson, spinning his last red-yellow-orange piece of da Vinci candy on the workbench. "How did your brain block out Edison's so you could let Klank know how to destroy the Edison BrainWaver and BrainWasher?"

"By canceling Edison's incoming beta brain waves with your more powerful gamma waves?" guesses Klink.

Frank gives a half smile. "Something like that. I used my very superior brain-wave blocker. My . . ." Frank takes off his Mud Hens hat and from the inside pulls out a silver—

"Hot dog wrapper?" says Watson.

"Tinfoil!" says Janegoodall. "Genius."

"To block all incoming brain waves," says Einstein.

Watson smacks his forehead. "So you were just pretending to be brain-controlled!"

"Exactly."

"Well, I'm just glad Edison didn't make us do anything weird or embarrassing while he was controlling us."

Einstein looks at his pal Watson.

"Er . . . right," Einstein lies.

Grampa Al tries another wire on the workbench project. Nothing.

"Son of a biscuit! So much good news— you got the BrainTurbo back, Janegoodall made starting pitcher, and, Watson, your 'all taste' da Vinci candy almost works."

Watson flicks his last candy into the wastebasket. "Nah. It's pretty disgusting. It turns out that mashing every taste together makes one big, bad taste."

Grampa Al nods. "Success is learning from failure." He rests his hand on the big metal torso on the bench.

"But I'm sorry to say this is a failure. We just can't fix it. We can't put Klank back together this time. That super-turbocharged brain pulse fried everything beyond fixing."

Nobody says anything.

The clock in Grampa Al's shop ticks off the seconds.

"Klank knew exactly what was going to happen," says Frank. "But he did it anyway. To save us." Frank puts his hand over the robot's old, motionless mannequin hand.

Janegoodall picks up a mannequin head. "I'm glad that Klank at least got his wish to be more human."

Frank absentmindedly taps a small screwdriver on his new notebook. "Klank was a great robot . . . but he's gone. And the rest of us have to keep going."

"Bleh," says Watson. "Why bother?"

Frank thinks. "Because we need to know," he says. "We need to know about all life. About all living things. How everything is connected. And how even death is part of all that."

The shop clock ticks, very loudly.

28

WHAT DO YOU SAY?" FRANK EINSTEIN ASKS.

No one says anything.

Everyone misses Klank.

"Klank would keep going. And I think he would want us to do the same," says Watson very quietly. "I'm with you, Einstein."

"We are all still functioning," Klink adds. "I am with you."

Grampa Al takes off the BrainTurbo and sets it on a spare intake hood. "Oh yeah. I'm in like Flynn."

"I'm in, too," says Janegoodall.

No one feels like moving. No one feels like saying anything else.

But something moves, and something speaks. A familiar voice, from an unfamiliar head, suddenly says, **"I am in, too!"**

Klank's arms reach out, pick up the intake hood, and plant it firmly on Klank's shoulders. Klank sits up.

"And I am in with a bigger and better head!"

"Klank!" yells Watson.

"Hug!" booms Klank.

Watson squeezes Klank in the biggest, longest, warmest human-robot hug ever.

"It is very interesting how you managed to connect a new head," beeps Klink, almost complimenting Klank.

"Yes, I missed you, too," bleeps Klank, pulling Klink into the hug.

"Your brain . . . ," says Frank. "Is it still . . . ?"

Klank instantly answers, **"E = mc², meaning energy is equal to mass times the speed of light squared."**

"You are still smart!" says Watson.

"Ha-ha-ha," laughs Klank. **"Just kidding. I read all that off the Wall of Science. Ha-ha-ha."**

Everyone laughs.

"But!" beeps Klank, **"I did learn something very important."**

"What?" asks Frank.

"I learned why the human skeleton did not cross the road."

"Why?" asks Klink.

"Because it did not have the guts. Ha-ha-ha-ha-ha-ha-ha-ha-ha-ha-ha-ha!"

MATTER

ENERGY

HUMANS

aristotle

E=mc²

newton

Tesla

da Vinci

"Whaaaaa? . . . bzzzt . . . eeeeeee!" bleeps Klink.

"Ha-ha-ha-ha-ha-ha-ha-ha-ha-ha-ha-ha."

"To life!" cheers Grampa Al.

"To life," cheers Frank Einstein, looking at his Wall of Science and filling up with a serious overload of happy feelings for all the goodness in his life.

"To . . . life!"

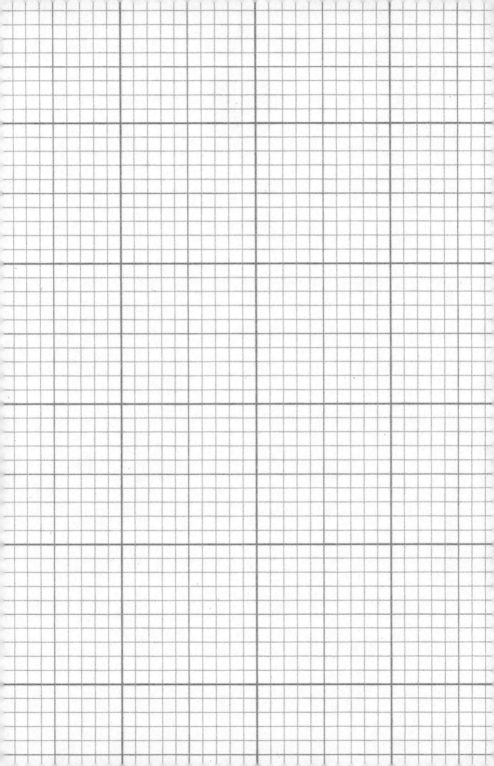

FRANK EINSTEIN'S
HUMAN-BODY NOTES

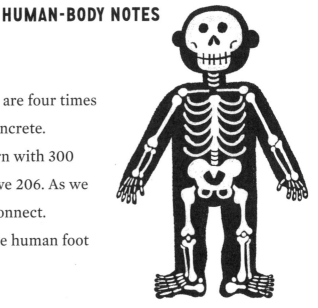

SKELETAL SYSTEM

Human bones are four times stronger than concrete.

Babies are born with 300 bones; adults have 206. As we age, our bones connect.

26 bones in the human foot alone.

MUSCULAR SYSTEM

200 muscles to take one step.

Average person takes about 10,000 steps in one day.

Smallest muscle is in the middle ear.

Eye muscle moves 100,000 times a day.

Heart muscle never stops.

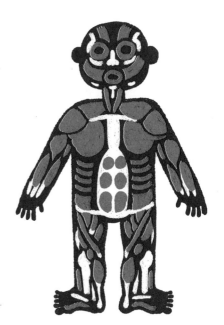

NERVOUS SYSTEM

Nerve impulses travel to and from the brain at speeds of up to 250 mph.

Brain generates enough power to light a 10-watt bulb.

Brain itself does not have nerves, therefore it cannot feel pain.

Brain uses 20 percent of the oxygen that enters our bodies.

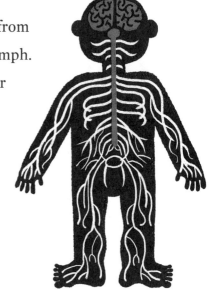

DIGESTIVE SYSTEM

Hardest part of the human body is tooth enamel.

Stomach makes a whole new lining for itself every three to four days.

In a lifetime, humans eat and digest about 60,000 pounds of food (about the weight of six whole elephants).

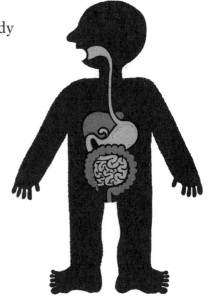

RESPIRATORY SYSTEM

Sneezes travel faster than 100 mph. Coughs, 60 mph.

Lungs inhale more than two million liters of air every day.

Nose warms cold air, cools hot air, and filters out impurities.

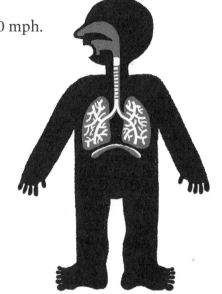

CIRCULATORY SYSTEM

Heart beats about 100,000 times a day, 35 million times a year, and 2.5 billion times in an average lifetime.

Red blood cells do a complete circuit of the body every 60 seconds.

In one day, a blood cell travels 12,000 miles (about the same as driving back and forth across the whole United States four times).

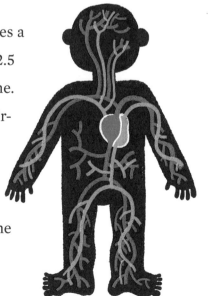

RANDOM BODY FACTS

Largest organ of the human body is the skin.

Humans shed forty pounds of skin in a lifetime, completely replacing the outer skin once a month.

It is not possible to tickle yourself.

Groove in upper lip is called a *philtrum*. No one knows why it's there.

Humans are about 75 percent water.

Human eyes do not grow. Noses and ears never stop growing.

Every human has a unique tongue print.

Teeth are the only part of the human body that cannot repair themselves.

Body contains hydrogen, oxygen, carbon. Also nickel, copper, silicon, and zinc.

The amount of carbon in a human body is enough to fill about 9,000 pencils.

Acid in stomach can dissolve metal.

Hair is almost indestructible.

Babies start dreaming before they are born.

PITCHING WITH JANEGOODALL

Good pitching starts with a good grip. Here is how to grip and throw the ball for three pitches you need to know.

CURVEBALL

The curveball spins in the opposite direction from the fastball—from top to bottom. This pitch curves down and in toward a right-handed batter.

- Grip the ball with your middle finger along the bottom seam of the baseball.
- Place your index finger alongside your middle finger.
- Position your thumb on the back seam.
- Throw this pitch snapping your middle finger down and pushing your thumb up.

FOUR-SEAM FASTBALL

This is a fast, straight, no-movement pitch. It spins from the bottom to the top.

- Grip the ball with your index and middle fingers across the two seams of the ball where they are widest apart.
- Place your thumb directly beneath your index and middle fingers, on the center of the seam at the bottom of the baseball.
- Hold the ball gently, as if you are holding an egg.
- Throw with maximum speed and backspin as you release the ball.

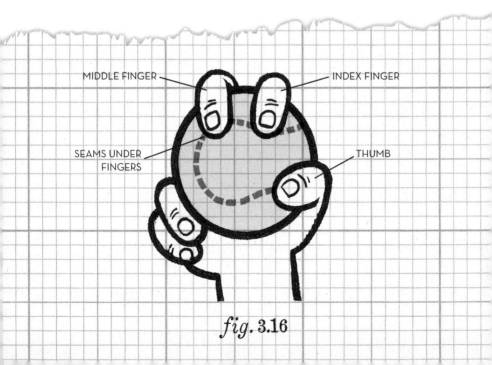

fig. **3.16**

KNUCKLEBALL

The perfect knuckleball spins with almost no rotation. That's what makes it move in strange and unpredictable ways.

- Press the fingernails of your index, middle, and ring fingers into the ball just behind the seams.
- Place your thumb under the ball, on the bottom seam.
- Pitch with a stiff wrist, pushing the ball toward home plate.
- Finish the pitch extending your fingers straight out, so the ball spins as little as possible.

WATSON'S INVENTOR CORNER

LEONARDO DA VINCI

Leonardo da Vinci was an artist, scientist, and inventor.
He was born in the town of Vinci in Italy in 1452.

His name just means "Leonardo of Vinci."

Leonardo invented early versions of the helicopter, parachute, tank, giant crossbow, flying machine, and scuba gear.
And a robotic knight.

Leonardo painted *The Last Supper* and the *Mona Lisa*.

Leonardo, like me, was left-handed, and he wrote a lot of his notes in mirror-image cursive—which made it very hard for people to figure out just how brilliant he was.

Leonardo's *Vitruvian Man* is a study on the proportions of the ideal human body. He believed that the human body revealed the universe. And so do I.

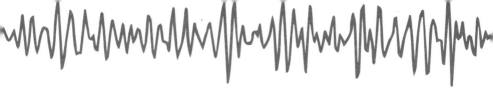

CLARENCE CRANE

In 1912, chocolate maker Clarence Crane of Garrettsville, Ohio, was looking for a sweet candy that wouldn't melt in the summer heat like his chocolate did.

Crane pressed mint candy into little round shapes with a hole in the middle that looked like tiny life-preserver rings.

So he called them Life Savers.

In 1935, cherry and pineapple flavors were added to the original lemon, lime, and orange . . . to make the classic Five Flavor Roll.

In 2003, Life Savers announced plans to add blackberry to the Five Flavor Roll. People freaked out. Life Savers returned to the classic five flavors.

Life Savers have been around for over 100 years.

The original roll cost 5¢.

Watson of Midville

BOB AND MARY EINSTEIN'S
TRAVELALLOVERTHEPLACE.COM
TRAVEL HOT SPOT!

THE MÜTTER MUSEUM

Philadelphia, PA

United States of America

★★★★★

If you love skulls and bones and brains and collections that are just a little creepy, you will love the Mütter Museum.

WHAT?

America's finest museum of medical history.

WHY?

The Mütter Museum's goal is to help visitors become "Disturbingly Informed."

HOW?

Amazing displays of anatomical specimens, models, and medical instruments.

WHO?

You . . . can see on display:

- Sections of Albert Einstein's brain!
- The Hyrtl Skull Collection. A collection of 189 skulls!
- A plaster cast of conjoined twins Chang and Eng and their livers!
- The Dr. Jackson Collection of 2,374 inhaled or swallowed foreign objects, including coins, buttons, beads, bolts, safety pins, screws, jewelry, keys, toy jacks, watch, crucifix, lock, bullet, thumbtacks, needles, keys, miniature horse charm, tiny binoculars, and so much more. Collected and lovingly cataloged by Dr. Chevalier Quixote Jackson (1865–1958).

WHAT WHAT?

The Mütter Museum Store sells: Conjoined-twin cookie cutters, glass skull drinking cups, human tooth jewelry.

WHERE?

19 S. 22nd Street
Philadelphia, PA
Muttermuseum.org

WHEN?

Monday–Sunday, 10 a.m. to 5 p.m.
Closed Thanksgiving, December 24–25,
January 1

KLANK'S TURING TEST

Alan Turing was a British computer scientist. In 1950, he made a test to consider the question, can machines think?

To find out if you are human or machine, answer the questions below.

A: Why did the duck cross the road?

B: Why did the monkey cross the road?

C: Why did the fish cross the road?

D: Why did the dog cross the road?

E: Why did the rooster cross the road?

For each correct answer, give yourself 1 point. If you score 3 or more points, you are probably human. If you score 2 points or less, you are most likely a machine.

"Wait, wait, wait a minute!" says Klink. "That is not the Turing test."

"It kind of is," says Klank.

"It is not."

"Well, it should be. Because it is very funny."

ANSWERS

A: He thought he was a chicken.

B: It was the chicken's day off.

C: To get to school.

D: To get to the barking lot.

E: To prove he wasn't chicken.

MR. CHIMP'S WORD SEARCH

B	R	A	I	N
O	A	P	E	A
O	T	E	P	P
S	D	E	A	E
T	U	R	B	O

APE	NEED	RAIN
(5 times)	PAN	RAP
BET	PAR	RAT
BOO	PEA	RUT
BOOST	PET	TAR
BRAIN	PI	TURBO

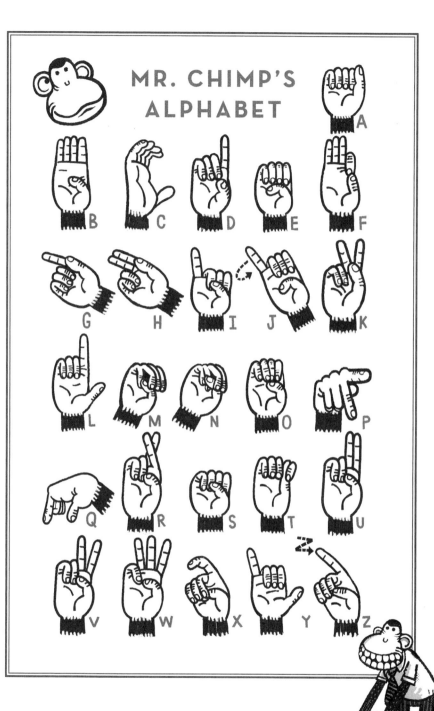

MR. CHIMP'S ALPHABET

JON SCIESZKA is composed of mostly oxygen, carbon, hydrogen, and a dash of magnesium. He started as a zygote, then became the author of a lot of books, the founder of Guys Read, and the first National Ambassador for Young People's Literature. He lives in Brooklyn, New York, and happily uses his body every day.

BRIAN BIGGS has illustrated books by Garth Nix, Cynthia Rylant, and Katherine Applegate, and is the writer and illustrator of the Everything Goes and Tinyville Town series. He lives in Philadelphia, pretty close to the Franklin Institute.

TO THE INSPIRATIONAL MRS. WATSON,
AND EVERY INSPIRING SCIENCE TEACHER

LIBRARY OF CONGRESS CATALOGING-IN-PUBLICATION DATA

SCIESZKA, JON.

FRANK EINSTEIN AND THE BRAINTURBO / JON SCIESZKA ; ILLUSTRATED BY BRIAN BIGGS.

PAGES CM. —— (FRANK EINSTEIN ; 3)

ISBN 978-1-4197-1643-0 (HARDBACK) —— ISBN 978-1-61312-829-9 (EBOOK)

[1. ROBOTS——FICTION. 2. INVENTORS——FICTION. 3. HUMAN BODY——FICTION.

4. HUMOROUS STORIES. 5. SCIENCE FICTION.] I. BIGGS, BRIAN, ILLUSTRATOR. II. TITLE.

PZ7.S41267FRM 2015

[FIC]——DC23

2015004219

ISBN FOR THIS EDITION: 978-1-4197-2735-1

TEXT COPYRIGHT © 2015, 2017 JRS WORLDWIDE LLC
ILLUSTRATIONS COPYRIGHT © 2015, 2017 BRIAN BIGGS
BOOK DESIGN BY CHAD W. BECKERMAN

PRINTED AND BOUND IN U.S.A.

10 9 8 7 6 5 4 3 2 1

AMULET BOOKS ARE AVAILABLE AT SPECIAL DISCOUNTS WHEN PURCHASED IN QUANTITY FOR
PREMIUMS AND PROMOTIONS AS WELL AS FUNDRAISING OR EDUCATIONAL USE. SPECIAL
EDITIONS CAN ALSO BE CREATED TO SPECIFICATION. FOR DETAILS, CONTACT SPECIALSALES@
ABRAMSBOOKS.COM OR THE ADDRESS BELOW.

ABRAMS The Art of Books
115 West 18th Street, New York, NY 10011
abramsbooks.com

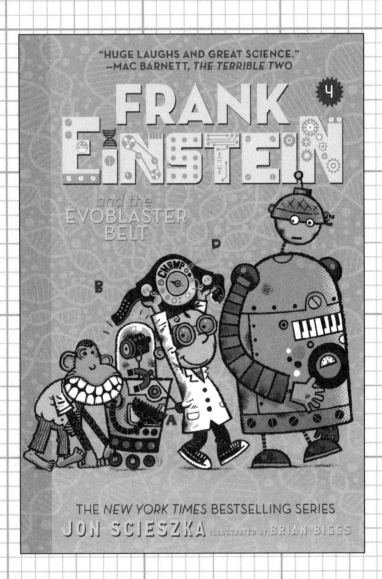

FRANK EINSTEIN
and the EVOBLASTER BELT

I

A **(A)** flaps its wings and . . .

. . . gets chomped in the jaws of a sticky-tongued green-and-black leopard frog **(B)** . . .

. . . that gets suddenly swallowed by a leaping largemouth bass **(C)** . . .

. . . that gets snagged by the sharp talons of a swooping red-tailed hawk **(D)** . . .

. . . that gets clawed by a jumping orange-and-white-striped house cat **(E)** . . .

. . . that gets chased through the woods by a barking hound dog **(F)** . . .

. . . that suddenly stops when it hears two humans yelling **(G)** . . .

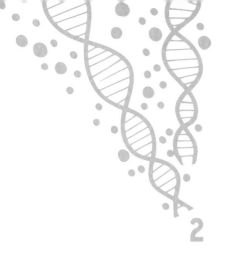

2

H

"Spin Kick!"

The hound dog stares at the two small humans battling each other in the meadow.

"Bear Hug!"

"Airplane Spin!"

The dog doesn't smell any food. It wonders what the humans are fighting over.

"Butt Drop!"

"Leg Lock!"

A bigger human appears at the edge of the clearing.

"Frank! Watson!" calls Grampa Al. "How about a little help putting up the tents?"

"Awww," says Frank Einstein.

"I totally had you pinned," says his pal Watson.

Frank releases Watson from his headlock. Watson releases Frank from his leg lock.

"And let's show some hustle!" calls Grampa Al. "Because Atomic Al wouldn't want to have to take you down with his Nuclear Piledriver." He bends forward, flexing his arms into a wrestling pose.

Watson looks at Frank in surprise. "Did he just say 'Atomic Al'? Does that mean your Grampa Al used to wrestle?"

Frank brushes the dirt and grass off his pants. "I never asked. But I would not be surprised."

"ATOMIC AL"

The hound dog snorts and trots off into the woods.

The orange-and-white-striped house cat, sitting safely high in a maple tree, licks its right paw.

Frank gives Watson his hand and helps him up. Watson picks his flashy gold championship-wrestling belt off a nearby bush and flips it over one shoulder. "This championship match will be continued later," says Watson.

Frank grabs the belt. "You were two seconds away from tapping out." He raises the belt overhead. "Woooooooorld Chaaaaampion—FFFFFrrrrraaaaaank EINSTEIN!"

Watson karate chops Frank and takes back the belt. "No way! I had you right where I wanted you."

The two guys laugh. They stop, stand in the middle of the meadow, and take in the sight of the sunlit clouds in a deep-blue sky overhead, the sound of a bee buzzing circles around the flowering clover, the smell of the pond behind them, and the trees all around them.

"How great is this?" says Watson. "Deep woods. Pure vacation. Nothing to do but goof around and relax."

Frank looks at the bee, the flower, the hawk overhead, the cat perched up in the tree. He sees something different. "It's relaxing for us. Because we are the top of the food chain. But look around, Watson. We forget that we are part of all this. Everything living is connected.

"And it's kind of perfect this is Darwin State Park. Because it was scientist Charles Darwin who called life the Struggle for Existence. Every minute of every day—eat or be eaten."

"OK, that's depressing," says Watson. "But at least we get a vacation from that sneaky T. Edison and his evil Mr. Chimp. And we get to go fishing."

Frank whacks Watson's championship belt. "Because we are *kings of the food chain.*"

"And it's good to be the king."

"And it's good to relax for a change, and not have to fix emergencies . . ."

The guys walk through the meadow and hop the stream toward the tents.

A bang, splintering wood, a yell, a crash, the *whoooop whoop whoop* of a siren split the sunset calm of the woods.

"Spoke too soon," says Frank.

He and Watson run for the tents.

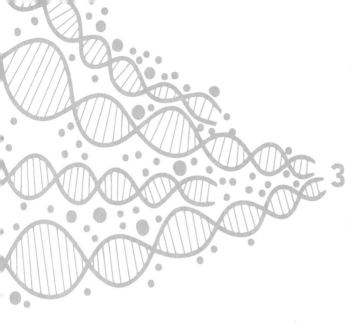

3

WEEEEEE-OOOOOO, WEEEEEE-OOOOOO, WEEEEEE-OOOOOOOO!" wails something in the middle of the Darwin State Park woods. "Yaah! Hooo! Haaah!" Wild yells add to the din.

A startled flock of crows explodes into the sky, flapping and cawing.

Frightened squirrels, rabbits, and field mice run, hop, scramble for safety.

Frank and Watson stop at the edge of the campsite and see where all the noise and commotion is coming from—a gigantic pile of dead tree branches jumping and shaking and howling.

Right where their tents used to be.

"WEEEEEE-OOOOOOO, WEEEEEE-OOOOOOO, WEEEEEE-OOOOOOO!"

"Yaah! Hooo! Haaah!"

"Oh man," says Watson. "Maybe we are not the kings of the food chain after all. Something *huge* is eating our tents!"

Frank picks up a hefty broken tree branch and swings it like a club. "And it's attacking Grampa Al! We have to save him! Come on!"

"Wait! What if it's Bigfoot?!"

"Then you can use your Head Butt."

Frank charges down the hill toward the thrashing, howling pile of craziness.

"Look big!" yells Frank. "And noisy! And mean!"

"WEEEEEE-OOOOOOOO, WEEEEEE-OOOOOOOO, WEEEEEE-OOOOOOOO!"

"Yaah! Hooo! Haaah!"

Frank and Watson jump on the pile of branches.

"We'll save you, Grampa!" yells Frank.

He smashes the branches covering the tents. "Take that!"

Watson head butts whatever it is under the tent fabric. "Owwwwwwww."

"WEEEEEE-OOOOOOOO, WEEEEEE-OOOOOOOO, WEEEEEE-OOOOOOOO!"

"Yaah! Hooo! Haaah!"

Something grabs Frank, wrapping him in a crushing python grip.

Frank kicks and struggles, but he can't move.

Watson rolls on the ground, holding his aching head.

"WEEEEEE-OOOOOOOO, WEEEEEE-OOOOOOOO, WEEEEEE-OOOOOOOO!"

"Yaah! Hooo! Haaah!"

The mess of branches, leaves, and wiggling tent suddenly blows apart.

And Frank and Watson see the monster that has been making all the noise.

"WEEEEEE-OOOOOO, WEEEEEE . . . oh . . . ," screeches a small robot.

"Klink!" says Frank.

"Yaah! Hooo . . . oops," says Grampa Al, still punching and kicking, with his glasses knocked sideways.

"Fighting with Grampa Al?" says Watson.

Frank turns to look at the Bigfoot holding him. But it is not Bigfoot. "Klank? What are you guys doing?"

"Grampa Al told me to get a lot of wood," answers Klank.

Grampa Al adjusts his glasses. "I probably should have been more specific about not delivering *a whole tree*. I thought we were under attack. I went into defense mode. And then Klink started freaking out."

Klink straightens his webcam. "I was not '*freaking out.*' The force of the falling plant life activated my new security alarm."

Klank lowers Frank to the ground.

"Darn," says Watson. "I thought we had found Bigfoot."

Grampa Al looks up at the setting sun. He calculates that they have about another half hour of good daylight. "We've got something bigger than Bigfoot. We've got a mission that has come from the Very Top."

"Ohhh, nice!" says Watson, pulling out his magnifying glass. "A secret spy mission? What is it? What is it?"

Grampa Al pulls the collapsed tent out of the pile of

branches. "Let's get our tents up first. Then I'll answer all your questions."

"Oooo! Oooo!" beeps Klank. **"I have a question. How can you tell if an elephant has been in your refrigerator?"**

Klink spins his head around in an annoyed twirl. "*What? This better not be one of your illogical jokes.*"

"Hmmmmmmm?" buzzes Klank.

"Because I do not want to hear something that does not make sense. That makes me burn out my brain circuits."

Watson laughs. "Well, I'd like to know. How *can* you tell if an elephant has been in your refrigerator?"

"If you see elephant footprints in the butter."

Watson cracks up laughing.

"Ha. Ha. Ha."

"Bzzzzzzzrrrrrrr," says Klink. "No! That cannot be true. Bzzzzzzz." Klink's brain circuits try to make sense of an elephant in a refrigerator. Klink's brain circuits start to overheat.

Watson laughs harder.

"Ha. Ha. Ha."

"Elephant . . . refrigerator . . . footprints . . . nooooooooooooo!"

Phooomp!

Klink blows a brain circuit and shuts down.

"Aw shoot," says Frank. "I wish you guys wouldn't do that. Now we have to reboot Klink. Again."

Grampa Al claps his hands. "OK! Let's get cracking! Tents up. Then I'll tell you what we are really doing here."

Crickets begin to chirp.

An owl hoots.

"Because we are not here just for the camping . . ."

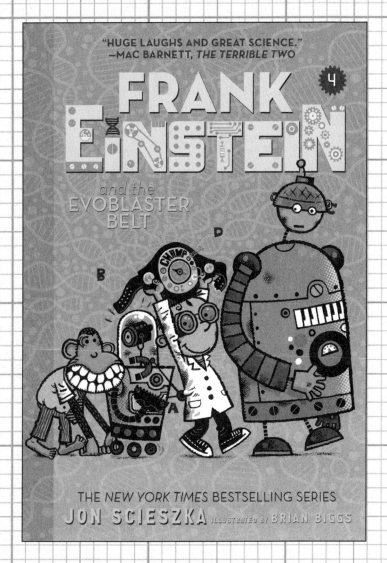